The
Alphabet Network

Jeanette Bresnihan was born in the West of Ireland. She was educated in Dublin, and after getting married she travelled overseas with her husband. After twenty-five years abroad, she has returned to Rosses Point in Sligo, where she lives with her husband, two cats, a parrot and a dog. She is a mother and a grandmother.

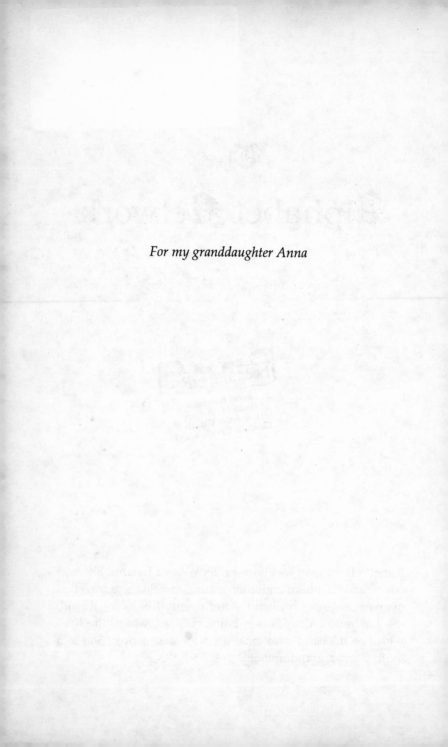

For my granddaughter Anna

The
Alphabet Network

Jeanette Bresnihan

WOLFHOUND PRESS

First published in 2000 by
Wolfhound Press Ltd
68 Mountjoy Square
Dublin 1, Ireland
Tel: (353-1) 874 0354
Fax: (353-1) 872 0207

The Arts Council
An Chomhairle Ealaíon

Wolfhound Press receives financial assistance from the Arts
Council/An Chomhairle Ealaíon, Dublin, Ireland.

British Library Cataloguing in Publication Data
A catalogue record for this book is available from the British Library.

ISBN 0-86327-833-7

10 9 8 7 6 5 4 3 2 1

Cover image: Photonica
Cover design: Wolfhound Press
Line drawings: Aileen Caffrey
Typesetting: Wolfhound Press
Printed in the UK by Cox & Wyman Ltd, Reading, Berks.

Chapter One

Katie opened her eyes. Outside everything was grey, so it didn't matter that the train was going too fast for her to see anything clearly. The view looked exactly the same as the view from her bedroom window: clumps of dried shrubs; lonely tree-trunks, their branches stretched towards her like begging arms; and the blur of grey-brown earth. She spotted a deserted farmhouse. She remembered her father telling her that people had once lived on farms like that, raising animals and growing crops.

'Crops, crops, crops....' Katie repeated the word to herself, tapping her finger in time on the pane.

Tom released his nose from the window.

'What's that funny word, Katie? Crops?'

Katie looked at her brother's pointed little face, his straggly hair and thin hands. *I'm going to take care of him forever, forever and ever and ever.* Her skin felt goose-bumpy — *A goose walking over my grave, that's what Dad used to say....*

'Katie, what are crops?'

Katie shivered and pushed her hair behind her ears. Her large brown eyes softened and she squeezed Tom's hand.

'They're ... they're things that grow in the ground — plants. They're green and you can eat them. Don't you remember, Daddy used to tell us about them? There were still some growing when he was a boy. He used to talk about delicious round things called potatoes — they grew in the ground, with flowery tops, and you had to dig them up.'

'Hmm,' Tom sighed. 'I'd love something to eat now. I'm hungry — all this talking about crops, crops, crops is making me hungry.'

Katie groaned. Once he started, he wouldn't stop.

'All right, then.' She fished a packet out of her bag. 'You can have a biscuit — just one, because they have to last the rest of the journey.' She slid along the metal seat. 'Here; not another word. We have a long journey to make, and we're not even sure where we're going.'

The frightened look on Tom's face made Katie feel like swallowing the words right back again. She hugged him. 'Don't worry, Tom. It'll be all right. I'll look after you, always. I promise.'

She was interrupted by a sharp, reedy voice. It made her start.

'Oh, what have we here? Don't often get the likes of you on my train. Few and far between, nowadays. I'd be careful if I was you. There's lots of folk who'd be mighty interested in two young 'uns — not being able to have any, like; you know what I mean. Now why would your mum be so careless as to send you out on your own? It would serve her right if something was to happen to you.' The ticket collector made a clicking noise with his tongue.

Katie could see Tom's eyes filling up. She could also see that he was about to say something, so she slid her foot along the floor and gave him a kick.

The ticket collector was standing with his head held at that inquisitive angle that people have when they want some information. Katie swallowed.

Putting on her most grown-up voice, she said, 'Well, actually, we're going to visit our grandfather.'

Then she pressed her lips tightly together. That was all he was going to learn.

'Hmph....' The ticket collector was obviously disappointed at his failure to extract more information.. 'Well, there you are — tickets checked. Mind yourselves.' He shook his head fiercely and shoved the punched tickets back at Katie. 'Here, you might as well have these.' He handed her a pack of playing cards. 'Now, if I were your parents, I'd keep you locked up!'

'Ugh,' whispered Tom. 'I'm glad he's gone, even if he did give us the cards. I didn't like him, Katie; he was creepy. He reminded me of the bogeyman, the one with the enormous bag who creeps around at night collecting children....'

Katie hugged him. 'That was only a fairy tale. But all the same, we should be careful. There are so few of us. We're so lucky to have each other....' Katie tried to stop her voice trembling. 'Remember, at school there weren't any other brothers or sisters — we were the only ones.' She drew Tom close to her, as much for her own comfort as for his. 'Look, aren't they lovely cards, though?'

They were nice: they were made of stronger plastic than Tom's old cards, and their designs were beautiful. Looking at them, Tom smiled in spite of himself.

'Come on,' said Katie, 'let's have a sleep. We've a lot of travelling in front of us.'

So, nestling together as comfortably as they could, they closed their eyes and slipped into a much-needed sleep.

જી

When Katie woke up, she saw that they had two companions: a rather pinched-looking woman and a thin-faced boy of about six. They were staring at Katie and Tom. The little boy's eyes were huge; he was staring intensely, as if he had never seen other children before. His mother, too, looked at Katie and Tom with puzzlement, amazed to see children travelling on their own.

'Hello,' said Katie shyly. She slowly stretched. 'That's better. We needed that, didn't we, Tom?'

Tom yawned and rubbed his eyes. He threw a quick glance at the boy and said, 'But now I'm hungry again. Have we got any more of those biscuits?'

A little hand shot out from across the table and pushed a packet of sweets towards Tom. The boy's mother nodded encouragingly. 'Go on, have a few.'

Katie smiled. This woman wouldn't be inquisitive — curious in the normal sense, yes, but not like the ticket collector. She'd probably just like to know why they were travelling on their own.

She found herself saying, 'I'm Katie, and this is my brother Tom. We're going to visit our grandfather....'

Once she started, she couldn't stop; it all came out in a rush. There was something about the woman's face. It was round, with a button nose and a smiley mouth, but there were lots of lines under her greeny-blue eyes. 'We're going to live with our grandfather because our dad just died, and our mum died when Tom was born.'

She could see the woman's eyes misting over. 'I'm so sorry. You poor things, all alone in the world.'

'Well, we do have each other,' said Katie.

'Oh yes, indeed you do. I would have loved another baby, but it isn't to be. Of course, I'm so blessed to have Jack. So many ... so many can't. I'm one of the lucky few.' She shook her shoulders and smiled. 'We're so lucky to have met you. What a treat for Jack! Do you realise that you're the first children he's ever met?'

'Well, Jack....' Katie began to rummage in her bag. 'I bet you'd like to play a game of cards with us.'

Jack nodded, and Tom grinned.

'How about Snap?'

కు

For the next hour of the train journey, the carriage resounded with shrieks, laughter and loud explosions of Snap. Jack's mother, Jane, thought that the beseeching trees outside the carriage windows might hear the children's laughter, and she felt a sense of hope even amid that dead, grey landscape. Seeing what fun and delight Katie and Tom gave Jack, she felt happier than she had in years.

'Oh, my dears, I wish....'

Her voice trailed off. Katie knew she wished that they belonged to her, that they could be a sister and brother for Jack. In a funny sort of way, Katie wished that as well; but she and Tom had to do something first — something really important.

కు

Katie looked out of the window and saw that the sky was becoming lighter. They must be near their destination, Liverpool.

She shut her eyes and gave a silent cry. *If only we could stay on the train, with Jack and his mother, for just a little longer!* She felt as if they were a real family: Jack was her little brother, and Jane, whose face had softened and relaxed, was her mother. Katie couldn't remember her own mother very well — she had only been seven or eight when she died — but she thought she must have looked like Jane.

Katie's dreaming was suddenly shattered by the ticket collector's voice: 'Ten minutes to Liverpool. We are due to enter the station in ten minutes, so please have your bags ready.' He winked at Katie. 'See you've got company. Now remember what I said.'

When he had gone, Tom stuck his tongue out. Katie explained to Jane what had happened earlier.

'I expect he's another that couldn't have any children. He was just taking it out on you two.' Jane took Katie's hand. 'He was right in a way, you know. You really must be very careful. There are some very nasty people out there who would do anything for money; and one of the easiest ways of making a lot of money nowadays is in the child market. Make sure you go straight to your grandfather's house when you get off this train. I expect there will be someone to meet you.'

Katie bit her lip. She wished she could tell Jane the truth about where they were going, but her father had made her promise to tell no one. She couldn't trust anybody, no matter how nice they were.

'Yes, of course.' She turned her eyes away from Jane's.

'Mummy, why can't they stay with us? We'd have such fun! Tom, show me that trick again....'

So the last few minutes of their train journey were spent in the most agreeable way. It was as if they were in a little bubble, separated from the grey, decaying world that sped by outside the windows.

'Liverpool, Liverpool. All out at Liverpool....' And there they were.

'Goodbye, my darlings.' Jane hugged Katie tightly.

'Jack, remember the card tricks I showed you,' said Tom. 'And when we see each other again.... We will, won't we, Katie — we will see them again?'

Katie looked away. 'You never know, Tom. But we have to say goodbye now.' She glanced around as if she were looking for someone. 'Bye, Jane — bye, Jack.... Come on, Tom.' And off they went, Tom throwing lingering glances back at Jane and Jack.

'Don't look back, Tom, it just makes it worse. Come on, we have to get to the docks — Dad said they were quite near the station.'

Tom was sniffing. 'I'm scared, Katie. I want to stay with them.' He rubbed his tears away with his sleeve and hopped from foot to foot.

Katie stopped, took him by the shoulder, and bent down so that she was looking straight into his eyes. She spoke in her most steely, headmistressy voice.

'Now look, Tom, you have to be strong. We're very lucky to be able to go where we're going. Most people don't even have the chance to go there, and we're going to *live* there. We have to be brave, though: it's a long journey, and remember, Dad asked us to do something very special and very important. You have to be like a soldier — we're on a secret mission!'

Tom clutched her for a moment and then drew himself up. He gave a long sniff. 'I'll try....' He was hopping even more. 'I have to do a wee!'

Katie looked around for a sign that said 'Toilets'.

'There's one over there — you see, straight across there. I'll stay right here. Come straight back.'

She put her rucksack on the ground and sat against it, all the time keeping an eye on the toilets. There were lots of people in the station, all dressed in drab grey and brown, as if they had forgotten what colours were. Quite a lot of them wore masks; they obviously hadn't bothered to remove them when they had come off the streets. There were no children, of course. The whole scene was spooky.

Katie looked at her watch. Where was he? Five minutes ... ten minutes.... She could feel her mouth getting dry and her palms becoming wet and clammy. A familiar gurgle began in her stomach. Her heart started to beat faster.

Oh, what could have happened? Should I go and look for him? But suppose he came out and saw I wasn't here.... What should I do?

Images flashed in front of her eyes: Tom a squirming figure in a sack, Tom lying on the cold toilet floor.... She could feel a cry rising in her throat.

Suddenly, out of the corner of her eye, she saw the ticket collector. He was whispering into the ear of a man — a very tall man in a mask, dressed in a white suit. The man in the white suit was resting his arm on the top of a conical cage. Its bars were made of very thin wood.

Katie stared at the cage. The bars danced before her eyes, and a boy's face swam in and out of them.... She stifled a scream.

The ticket collector was pointing at her. She shut her eyes. When she opened them, she was almost afraid to breathe.

She saw two figures — no, three — moving in her direction. Jane and Jack — yes, Jane and Jack with Tom between them, all three holding hands.

'Look what we found, Katie! Somebody came out of the wrong door!'

Katie ran towards them and clutched Tom, tears springing up in her eyes. 'I thought — I thought.... Oh, thank you ... thank you. What happened? Tom, why didn't you come straight out? I had my eye on the door all the time.'

Tom's bottom lip quivered. 'There was another door. It led out a different way, and then I couldn't see you, and there were all these people around.... And I saw that ticket collector —'

'He was with a man in a white suit. I know. I saw him as well.' Katie shivered.

'They were pointing at me. I was so scared.... And then Jane came.'

'The poor little mite was looking so lost — I couldn't understand what had happened,' said Jane briskly. 'Anyway, you're coming home with me. I don't know what's happened to the person who's supposed to be meeting you, but you certainly can't stay here in this ghastly station.'

∽

Jane and Jack lived in a flat over a shop somewhere in Liverpool. Their flat looked exactly the same as every other flat, except for the cushions dotted everywhere — and the books. They were torn and discoloured, but they were books.

Katie had only seen a book once before, and that had belonged to her dad. Here there were at least two shelves full. She stared at the worn spines, and the titles danced before her eyes: *David Copperfield*,

Jane Eyre, *The Thirty-Nine Steps*, *Lord of the Rings*, *Heidi*, *Gulliver's Travels*....

She felt a gentle hand on her shoulder.

'These are my treasures, Katie. They are very precious. Do you want to have one? Which one would you like?'

Katie took a deep breath. What a choice!

'*David Copperfield*, please. I once read it on the electronic library, and I loved it. Wow — I've never felt a page before.'

She reverently took the book from Jane, sat down and began to turn the pages. They felt funny, like a dead leaf she had once found. There was a warm, yeasty smell. She settled down and started to read.

&

That evening, while Tom and Jack played endless games of Snap and Tom taught Jack more of his tricks, Katie told Jane everything. She knew she could trust her, and she knew that if her father had been there, he would have felt the same.

'Dad was killed,' she said quietly. 'He was on an assignment, taking photographs. They said he fell off a cliff. We weren't at home; he'd sent us to stay with a friend. He knew something was going to happen. He gave us —' Katie stopped. She didn't want to tell Jane about the box. 'He gave us something for Grandfather.'

'Katie, you know that you can stay here as long as you like.' Seeing Katie shake her head, Jane added, 'Well, perhaps for a couple of days....'

'No, not even that, Jane. Thanks.' Katie was fighting her instinct to say yes. 'We must go. We have to get to Grandfather as soon as possible.'

Jane took the book from Katie, opened it to the front page and showed her a label with an address written on it.

'Keep the book and think of us; and you know where we are, just in case....'

Katie threw her arms around Jane.

'We'll see you again, I promise. But tomorrow we have to take the boat to Dublin.'

Chapter Two

'**S**upposing they won't let us through?' Tom was tugging at Katie's sleeve.

'Shh — stop it!' Katie was feeling nervous. She bit her lip and tried to look calm. 'We'll be all right, Tom.' She hugged him. 'I'm sorry for being horrible to you; it's just....'

Tom squeezed her hand. 'Don't worry, Katie. Daddy said there'd be no problems; all our papers are in perfect order.'

Inch by inch, their queue moved forward, nearer and nearer to the desk where a man and a woman examined papers. It seemed to take ages. The officers were both dressed in the same dark-green uniform. They wore black berets, and Katie noticed a gold shamrock badge glinting in the light.

Drifts of conversation floated around her and Tom.

'... waited five years for this....'

'... very difficult....'

'... won it in a quiz....'

'... years onto our lives ... air, food....'

Inch by inch — only six people in front of them.... Tom tugged at Katie.

'Katie, your hand is all slippy.'

'Shh. It's all right, it's only a little sweaty. That happens when —'

Two shiny black shoes stopped beside them. A

hand tapped Katie's arm. She looked up to see a stern-faced woman with cold eyes and red cheeks. Her dark hair was swept back under a black beret. She had a clipboard in one hand; Katie could see a list of names, some of them circled in red. She took a deep breath and smiled her sweetest smile.

'Yes?'

A metallic voice, more like a man's, asked, 'Are you Katherine and Thomas Kenny?'

Katie and Tom nodded.

'You are travelling to Ireland?'

They nodded again.

'Reason for visit?'

'Holiday.' They both said it together — a little too eagerly, perhaps.

'Hmm. Unusual to have two children travelling alone ... most unusual.'

The woman stood with her head to one side, pen dangling in the air.

Katie looked straight into her eyes. 'Our parents are dead. We're visiting our ... our relatives.'

'Hmm....' The woman looked at her clipboard for a minute, then at the impatient faces behind Katie. 'All right, then. I expect your papers are in order.'

Katie nodded. The woman ticked their names and strode off.

Katie felt like a balloon when its air escapes. She let out a huge breath.

'Katie, why didn't you say that we're going to stay with Grandfather?'

'Because, Tom....' Now that the danger was over, Katie was feeling oddly elated. 'Because Daddy said we weren't to tell anyone about Grandfather; it's too dangerous.'

'Papers, please!' They were standing in front of

the immigration officers. The female officer smiled at them. She had the loveliest skin Katie had ever seen; it shimmered, and her eyes looked like two blue pools. 'Hello there. Going to Ireland for a holiday?'

Tom nodded.

'Is this your sister?'

Tom nodded again.

The other officer, who looked very serious, frowned as he riffled through their passports, health cards....

'Hmm.... Sorry about your father. Must have been tough, though it happens all the time here. You'll see a different world across the Irish Sea, I can tell you that!' He smiled kindly at them. 'Make the most of your two weeks, now, d'ye hear? Get some colour into those cheeks. Go on now. Take care.' He gave Katie an enormous wink as he handed her back their papers.

᳇

Katie and Tom ran down the stairs to the hovercraft as if all the demons in the world were after them. They climbed on board and sank gratefully into their seats.

'I want to sit beside the window,' said Tom, but his face fell when he saw that the windows had been painted over.

Katie was packing her bag away in the overhead locker.

'I think that's because they don't want any of us to see the way.' She felt light and happy, now that they had passed the first obstacle of their journey. She laughed. 'Just in case we might swim over!'

The hovercraft was soon under way, and in no time at all a soft, melodious voice came through the sound system:

'Welcome to Ireland. *Céad míle fáilte* — a hundred thousand welcomes. You are about to have the privilege of setting foot on our ancient land. A land here since the beginning of time, bathed in mists. A land whose shores are lapped by the life-giving waters of the Atlantic. Air that you can breathe awaits you; water gushes into our lakes from fern-shrouded waterfalls. And now, here is our Minister for Finance and Tourism, Séamus Slevin, to say a few words.'

The melodious voice was replaced by the deeper, flatter voice of the Minister. 'Yes, indeed, you are very privileged, and we hope that you enjoy your short stay in this great little country of ours. Eat, drink, breathe, and add years to your life.'

This was followed by a blast of Irish music. Katie and Tom were familiar with the mournful sound of the uilleann pipes and the rhythmic thumping of the bodhrán; their father had played music all the time. But now it sounded different, as if it belonged here, as it had never belonged in the grey, barren landscape of their home.

Katie noticed that their fellow passengers were already looking brighter. She looked at Tom. His cheeks did look a little pinker, but his eyes still had that frightened-rabbit look.

She squeezed his arm. 'Everything's going to be all right. Remember, Dad told us about contacts. We're not on our own; we'll have people to help us.'

∞

At Immigration, there were people in the same kind of uniform that the officials in England had worn — black berets and green uniforms — but they only gave the passengers' documents a cursory glance; the real checking had taken place at the other end.

A beautiful girl with long red hair curling down to her waist smiled at Katie and Tom. 'Welcome to Ireland, you poor wee things. You look in real need of some fresh air. You'll be met by your relatives out there.'

Katie smiled shyly at her, and they walked on in the direction the girl had indicated. *If only she knew*, Katie thought. If only she knew that there weren't any relatives, and that their only connection lived somewhere at the other side of the country — Katie didn't even know where.

ထ

Tom and Katie stood outside the terminal, blinded. Tom was screaming.

'Katie, I can't see! What's happening? Everything's gone black!'

Katie put out her hand. 'Hold on to me, Tom! I don't know — I don't know....'

Then a voice said, 'Ah, sure, it's only the sun. You're not used to it — sure, you've probably never seen it before. Ye should have been warned. Now keep your eyes shut for a minute, then open them slowly. One, two, three ...'

Katie counted, 'Four, five, six ...' Tom was joining in: 'Seven, eight....'

The voice came again. 'Now open them, very slowly.'

Katie did as she was told. There in front of her

eyes were people — all kinds of people in brightly coloured clothes. She blinked again. She could see the sky, she could see for miles and miles — it was as if the air was a magnifying glass. And there were trees scattered here and there on the streets, trees surrounded by green — it must be grass....

She gasped, 'This is so beautiful!'

Tom was gasping and coughing.

'Tom — Tom, are you all right?'

The same voice came again. 'Don't worry, my dear, this always happens. It's the air, you see; you're not used to it. Sure, his poor lungs haven't experienced anything like it.'

The voice belonged to a round, middle-aged man with a shiny brown head lapped by a little fringe of grey hair. He had twinkly blue eyes and red cheeks. *Everyone has red cheeks in Ireland,* Katie thought.

'Now where do you two come from? You're not from Ireland, that's for sure!'

Katie thought for a moment. Her father had warned her about his enemies. *'Now remember, don't trust anyone. These people are masters of disguise. You'll be given a code soon after you arrive, but in the meantime, don't tell anyone* — anyone — *your business.'*

'We're here on holiday, actually. We're going to stay with a relative.'

The little man gave a satisfied cough. 'Sure, amn't I right: you're strangers. Well, you'll probably be needing to go somewhere. I've got a horse and trap — I'm a cabby. Come on.'

He took up their bags and waddled around the corner.

'Katie, Katie!' Tom was tugging at her. 'Remember what Daddy said?'

'Shh, Tom, it's all right. We're only going as far as Trinity College; that's our first contact point. We have to go to the library and ask to see the keeper of the Book of Kells.' She gave Tom a reassuring hug. 'I don't think anything much can happen to us between here and there.'

Chapter Three

'Gee-up!' The cab-driver tugged the reins and gave his horse a little tap with his whip, and they were off. Clippity-clop, clippity-clop....

There was something reassuring about the sound of the horse's hooves; there was also something that made Katie and Tom drowsy. In no time at all, they had their eyes shut. The cabby, who was talking to his horse, didn't notice until he turned around to say something and heard nothing but gentle snores.

He shook his head and smiled to himself. 'Ah, the poor wee things ... they shouldn't be out on their own at all, at all. That wee girl seems older than her years. She needs a bit of relaxin', she does. Gee-up there, Sally, gee-up.'

&

Katie and Tom emerged from their sleep with the smell of the sea in their noses and the taste of salt on their lips. Katie rubbed her eyes and looked around. She saw a long strand on her right, with a flat, calm sea stretching to the horizon. The sea was very far out, and the strand seemed to go on for miles. There were lots of birds — white, grey, tiny and big — all looking for food.

'Tom, look! Look at those birds — all kinds!'

The cabby turned around. 'Oh, ye're awake. The clip-clop always puts my passengers to sleep. Have ye never seen seabirds before? Sure, of course ye wouldn't, over there. Do you see the group of black-and-white ones with long yellow beaks, pecking in the sand by the water's edge? They're called oyster-catchers.'

'What are those tiny little grey birds with the long legs, hopping about?' asked Tom.

'They're sanderlings.'

'Oh, they're all so beautiful!' Katie and Tom said in chorus, and the cabby smiled broadly.

Katie sniffed. 'The air is so different.'

'That'll add years onto your life,' said the cabby. 'Everyone lives to a great old age in this country. Pity ye're only here for a visit.'

Katie saw that Tom was about to say something, so she gave him a quick kick. 'We're going to make the most of it.'

As the cabby nodded, Katie heard a peculiar cracking sound coming from underneath her seat. She was sitting on the right side of the cab, just over the wheel. She hadn't heard that sound before.

Crack.... Tom heard it too. It was getting louder. *Creak....*

'Excuse me....' Katie tried to get the cabby's attention. 'Excuse me.' She tapped him on the back.

He turned around and smiled at her.

'By the way, my name is Martin. Is it another bird that you want to know about?'

Then he saw from the look on her face that it was more than that.

Katie pointed at the place where the sound was coming from. Martin nodded and tugged at the reins.

'Whoa there, Sally. Good girl.' The cab came to a stop. 'All right now, children, out ye get.'

Martin had stopped the cab at the side of the road, close to a grassy bank; the other side of the bank sloped down to the strand.

'Hmm.' He examined the wheel. It was plain to see where the noise was coming from: one of the wooden spokes had splintered.

Martin shook his head. 'It was a near thing, and it's lucky you two have sharp ears as well as sharp eyes. I'll have to take off this wheel and see if I can fix it. I hope ye're not in a hurry.'

Katie shook her head. They weren't really; and for some reason she felt safe with this man.

'Right, hop over that bank and have a play in the sand while I fix this.'

Tom was delighted that this had happened; he was beginning to get fidgety.

'Race you, Katie!' And up over the bank he went, tumbling down the slope, scrabbling in the sand as he tried to get as far ahead of Katie as he could.

Katie took her time. She carefully removed her sandals and tucked up her skirt, and then she was off — 'Katie-long-legs,' as her father used to call her. Sprinting along, she soon caught up with Tom. In fact, they both arrived at the water's edge at the same time, collapsing onto the sand and shrieking at the tops of their voices, 'I won, I won!'

Then they both lay still, flat on their backs, gazing up at the sky. It seemed to go on and on and on — blue as blue, with the occasional fluffy cloud sailing across.

'Mmm. I could stay here forever, just like this. You know, Tom, if you lie absolutely still you can feel the world turning.'

∞

They lay there for ages — or, at least, it seemed like ages; it was really only a few minutes. Then there was the sound of a car, and Katie heard voices — two voices; it wasn't just Martin talking to Sally. Some instinct warned her to lie as still as she could. Luckily, Tom seemed to have fallen asleep.

Snatches of words wafted down on the breeze: 'Two of them — girl and a boy.... No, not at all....'

Katie could feel the hairs prickling on the back of her neck, and her heart began to thud. *Surely not already!* She slid onto her stomach, slithered like a snake along the sand and up to the bank, and edged her head over the top.

A small black car was parked beside the cab. Martin was bent down, fixing the wheel and obviously talking to someone on the other side of the cab. Katie could see him making gestures with his hands.

She could also see a pair of white shoes — just shoes. She craned her neck to see more, but then the shoes began to move. Katie held her breath....

The shoes belonged to a pair of white trousers. Katie let out her breath, biting her lip to stop any sound coming out. It was the man in the white suit. She couldn't see his face, because he had his hat pulled down low.

Suddenly she thought of Tom. Suppose he woke up and shouted out! She backed away from the bank and turned around to see if Tom was still asleep. She shut her eyes and prayed: *Stay asleep, Tom!* Sometimes if she thought hard enough about something it happened.

Katie didn't think for one moment that Martin would give them away. She knew he would protect them. She scrambled back to the bank and glanced over; the black car had gone.

Katie put her head in her hands and took three deep breaths. Her knees felt like jelly and her stomach was doing somersaults, but for the moment she and Tom were safe.

'Hey, you two,' Martin was calling. Katie scrambled up over the bank and waved to him. He had fixed the wheel and was wiping his face with an enormous red hankie.

'Whoo — I'm glad that's fixed.'

He stood for a moment looking warily at Katie.

'What kind of friends do you have, anyway? Pretty peculiar, I'd say. While ye were down on the strand, this fellow — dressed all in white, if you don't mind — stopped and asked me if I'd seen you two and if I'd given you a ride. I didn't like the look of him, I can tell ye. Never seen such eyes before. No, I have: on a snake — snake-eyes was what he had. And what's a fella like him doing with a car? Sure, only officials and high-ups in the government drive cars. So I told a lie. I just had this feeling he was up to no good. He spun me a tale about him being your uncle and about you having run away. He got very annoyed when I told him I hadn't seen you at all. It was as if he'd seen you get up into the cab. So I says, "Oh, those two! Now I remember: I saw them getting into Mickey Brady's cab. They were heading down towards Heuston Station." That got rid of him.'

'Oh, thank you....' Katie wanted to hug him, but something in his face stopped her — a serious, stern look.

'Now, I don't know what the story is. I don't even know if you're going to stay with a relative. I don't know if I really want to know — there are some funny things goin' on in this country at the moment. All I do know is that you should take care. It's not safe for you and your brother to be out here alone.'

By now Tom had woken up and arrived at Katie's side, his face screwed up with sleep and anxiety; he knew that something had happened.

Martin ruffled Tom's hair. 'Hop in. I'm going to bring ye to Trinity College, for that's where ye want to go. I want ye to lie down under this rug' — he tossed a purply-red rug at them — 'just in case our friend comes sniffing after us again. Right, off we go! Are you two covered up?'

Katie and Tom snuggled under the rug, with just a chink to let the air in, and gave a muffled grunt.

'Gee-up. On you go, Sally, good girl.'

❧

Clip-clop, clippity-clop.... Was it Katie's imagination, or were they slowing down? She peeked out from under the rug and saw that they were travelling down a narrow street; occasionally someone riding a bicycle passed them, but otherwise the street was empty.

'Are you two all right back there?' Martin's voice was just above a whisper as he leaned over the rug. 'We're nearly there; we're just a few streets away from Trinity. I can't take you to the gate because the inner city is all pedestrianised, so you'll have to walk the last bit. I'm going to pull over to this side-street here and let you off. Whoa, Sally, whoa — there's a good girl.'

Katie shut her eyes for a moment. She wished she and Tom could stay under the rug forever. It was so cosy and safe.... She felt a tear beginning to form, and she shut her eyes even tighter to stop it rolling down her cheek. She had to be strong, and not just for Tom and herself. She remembered her father's last words to her: *'Katie, you must get the box to him. It's not just for your and Tom's safety, it's....'*

Katie put a hand into her back pocket and felt for the box. It was thin — hardly a box, really — and it fit into the palm of her hand.

Feeling the box gave her some courage. She pulled herself together and poked Tom.

'We're there. Come on!'

Martin helped them down from the cab and handed them their bags. His face looked worried and he was shaking his head.

'I don't like leaving ye like this. Are ye sure ye don't want to come home with me and have a good rest? There's something queer goin' on, I can feel it in my bones, and you two are mixed up in it somehow.'

Katie put out her hand. 'Martin, we'll be fine. You've been very kind to us, but we really are meeting someone in Trinity College — really. He'll see us on our way.'

Martin scratched his head. 'All right. But I'll tell you what: I have a young nephew who lives down the country, near the Shannon. He belongs to a traveller family — ye don't know what a traveller family is, I suppose. Travellers are descended from the ancient tribes of Ireland. They were thrown off their land hundreds of years ago and have never settled since. They know everything there is to know about the countryside and the animals that live in it. My grandparents used to be travellers, but they took the State's shillin' and settled down; but ye see I'm still on the road with my Sally. Now I'll give you my nephew's name.'

Martin took a pencil from behind his ear and wrote something down on a piece of paper.

'There you are — Rory Sweeney, Long Field, Ballymote, County Sligo. Ye can trust him with your lives. Just tell him I sent ye!'

He handed Katie the paper and then hugged them both, pulling the two of them in to his large belly. He patted them on their heads and said in a gruff voice, 'God bless ye, and have a safe journey, wherever ye're going. Now off ye go — straight down that street to the end, turn left, and you'll see Trinity College in front of ye.'

He got up onto his seat and tugged on the reins.

'Gee-up, Sally, gee-up....' And he was off.

Chapter Four

Katie and Tom stood for a moment and gazed through the arch, over the cobblestones, at the belltower in the middle of the square that was the heart of Trinity College. Crowds of people speaking all kinds of strange languages milled everywhere, and Katie and Tom were lucky to get a clear view of the tower.

Katie noticed that the tourists were in groups, and that each group was headed by a leader dressed in a smart green suit. There weren't any other people around, and Katie began to feel uneasy. One or two of the green-suits were looking over in their direction.

'We'd better go and look for Mr O'Brien — he's the man we've got to contact. I don't think we're meant to be here on our own like this, and we shouldn't draw attention to ourselves. Come on, let's attach ourselves to a group — this group here beside us. They're about to go into the college.'

Katie spotted a likely-looking man and woman who, she supposed, would be the right age to be their parents. She tugged Tom by his sleeve and they fell into step behind them. Occasionally the woman turned around and smiled at them in an awkward way. Luckily, they didn't have to chatter, as the green-suited man was doing all the talking.

Katie guessed that he was speaking some European language — not one that she was familiar with. She did pick up the odd word, and when she heard the words 'Book of Kells', her heart skipped a beat.

'Tom,' she whispered, 'we're going to see the Book of Kells! We don't have to go around searching for it; we're actually being brought in!'

Tom looked puzzled. Before he could say anything — and Tom didn't know how to whisper — Katie murmured, 'Mr O'Brien is the keeper of the Book of Kells!'

By now their group was under the campanile — Katie had picked up that word as well. The guide was pointing to various windows, and there were oohs and ahs from the group. Katie noticed that their 'mother' was becoming anxious about something; she kept poking her husband and whispering. Then he would look around and grin awkwardly.

Katie nudged Tom. 'We're going to have to slip away from this group as soon as we can. I think our "mother" is getting worried.'

'Look, we're nearly there.' Tom was pointing to a huge sign which had 'Book of Kells' written on it. 'Katie, they're collecting tickets! What will we do?'

Katie stopped and studied the scene in front of them. The entrance to the Book of Kells was on the left; just beside the entrance, on the right, there was a sign saying 'Toilets'.

'Okay, Tom, here's what we do — actually, what you do! I want you to do your toilet disappearing trick again. Here, take this envelope; it's got Mr O'Brien's name on it. Go to the toilet — run as fast as you can, look as if you're really bursting to go. After a few minutes, slip out of the toilet. Then, very quietly, squeeze into the queue, between the legs.

No one will notice; they're just thinking about not missing their turn. Once you're inside, go up to the desk and ask for Mr O'Brien. I'll wait here behind the pillar. Go on, off you go!'

Katie slipped behind the pillar, and Tom ran towards the toilets. She watched as he ran awkwardly, one hand clutching himself, the other waving in the air. He was certainly providing entertainment for the people in the queue. Some were shaking their heads, others were grinning, and some looked surprised — including the guide, whose eyes were darting between Tom and his 'parents'.

Hmm, thought Katie. *Safe for the moment, but not for much longer. I bet he's wondering where I've got to. Just as well Tom's nearly there.*

As Tom disappeared from view, she saw the guide moving towards her 'parents' and speaking into his walkie-talkie.

We haven't much time left. Katie felt her hands go clammy and her mouth turn dry. She peered around the pillar again. No sign of Tom, and her 'parents' were shrugging their shoulders and looking baffled as the guide spoke to them.

∞

In the meantime, Tom was preparing himself for the hardest part of his journey. Fortunately, he was totally unaware that the guide was getting suspicious. Luckily he was small and wiry, and he was also very good at playing invisible. He had a knack for disappearing; 'Where's Tom?' was a well-known cry.

He took a deep breath, pushed the toilet door open, got down on his hunkers and moved crabwise towards the nearest legs in the queue. He reckoned that he would have to slip through about six pairs of legs before he got to the door leading to the Book of Kells. Then he would just walk in casually, with the piece of paper in his hand: a messenger looking for Mr O'Brien.

Slowly, slowly, like an invisible crab, he moved. The tourists were all talking nineteen to the dozen in their strange languages. As Tom moved closer and closer to the legs, a blur of brown shoes, sandals, grotesquely misshapen toes, purple nails, and ugly wart-like growths swam before his eyes.

It was time to lie down on his stomach. He would slither through the gaps, being very careful not to bump too hard. The door was only about a foot away.

Oh please, legs, move apart, he prayed. The owner of the feet nearest the door seemed to be squeezing his legs together. *Move, move,* willed Tom.

And just as the voice above the legs began to sound puzzled, the legs separated and Tom was through — through the large doorway and into a dark interior.

Chapter Five

Tom pulled himself up against the wall and took a deep breath. He stood still for a moment, listening for clattering feet, in case someone had spotted him or the guide was running after him. There was nothing; just the sound of murmuring voices.

Tom carefully took the piece of paper out of his pocket and folded it to look like an envelope. He rubbed his face, patted his shirt and began to walk.

He was in a huge hall; its high-beamed ceiling created a kind of echo, so Tom could hear his own feet pattering along the floor. He was looking for a desk, or at least for some sort of sign that said 'Reception'. As the room was so dark and his eyes had been used to the brightness outside, it was difficult to see anything.

Tom was peering straight ahead when he felt a tap on his shoulder. He gulped and turned around. At first he could see no one; then he looked up into the face of one of the tallest men he had ever seen. The face itself was shaped like a triangle, topped with a strand of wirelike hair; two kind grey eyes gazed out from behind a pair of tiny spectacles.

'Well, my lad, what might you be doing in here on your own? Have you lost your parents?'

Tom nodded and then shook his head. He mustn't

get confused. He held out the envelope. 'I'm — I'm to
find Mr O'Brien ... give him a message....'

The long thin man smiled. 'Ah, it's Charlie you're
after. That's all right, then; I know where you'll find
him. Come with me.'

Tom let out a sigh of relief and trotted along after
the man's long, spindly legs. They moved across the
hall and along a corridor, dark and musty except for
the mote-laden light filtering through the windows.
They passed through an enormous wooden doorway
and entered the largest room Tom had ever seen —
a room that was filled to the brim with shelf upon
shelf of books. He stood transfixed, gazing up at the
rows and rows of volumes.

'Come on, lad. Haven't you ever seen books before?'

Tom was about to say 'No,' but then he remembered that he had seen books in Jane's flat. And
anyway, he supposed that Ireland was different
from England: there were still libraries in Ireland,
and lots and lots of books, so he shouldn't be
surprised. Instead he said, 'It's such a long room!'

'That's right, boy. It's known as the Long Room,
and we'll find our friend Mr O'Brien down at the end.'

Tom was running to keep up with the man's
stride. *He's like a spider!* Somehow Tom felt that he
could trust this man, and he knew already that
Spider and Mr O'Brien were good friends.

'Charlie, Charles....' Spider was calling as they
neared a desk — a high, old-fashioned, sloping
desk. Tom looked for Mr O'Brien, but all he could
see was the desk.

Suddenly he saw the top of a head, a head with
wispy, curly white hair. When the head lifted, Tom
saw that it belonged to a tiny man dressed in a
tweed suit, a waistcoat and a spotted bow-tie.

Mr O'Brien hopped down off his tall stool and held out his hand to Tom.

'Ah, my dear, I see that you have fallen into safe hands. I've been expecting you.' He glanced up at his tall friend. 'My friend Mr Moriarty always knows where to find me. Now, what have you got there?'

Tom handed him the envelope. 'It's just got your name on it, nothing else.'

Mr O'Brien took the envelope and opened it. He took out a piece of paper and laid it flat on his desk. 'Now, Tom, what do you think this is?'

Tom saw a picture of an eagle; below it were some jumbled letters and a picture of another animal — a wolf.

'It's a message in code.'

Mr O'Brien nodded. 'Good boy. Do you think you could work it out on your own?'

Tom stared at the letters.

MPPL BGUFS NZ DIJMESFO MJPO BXBJUT

Two pairs of eyes twinkled at him.

'Well, if ... if these letters stood for other letters in the alphabet ...' Tom bit his lip. 'I think I ...'

Mr Moriarty patted his head. 'We know you could, but we're short of time, so we'll do it instead. Let's see — if M equals L and P equals O....'

Tom looked on while the two heads bent over the piece of paper on the desk.

'Come here, Tom.' Mr O'Brien beckoned him over to the desk and showed him the message. 'You see, it's from your father. "Look after my children. Lion awaits." His code-name was Wolf.'

Tom still looked puzzled. 'Lion?'

Mr Moriarty removed his glasses and rubbed his nose. 'We'll explain later. But there should be another child....'

'Katie, that's Katie.' Tom rushed out the words. 'She's outside, hiding — just in case —'

Mr O'Brien pursed his lips and nodded. 'Quite right. They've got eyes and ears everywhere; we've got to be very careful. Now, Moriarty, how are we going to get the girl in here?'

Mr Moriarty sat down on a chair and crossed his long legs. 'I have to get into a thinking position.' He shut his eyes and folded his long arms behind his head.

Mr O'Brien put a finger to his lips in a shushing movement. He whispered to Tom, 'This always works. Just be patient for a few minutes. Katie will be all right.' He took a large round clock out of his pocket. 'I bet you've never seen one of these!'

Not only had Tom never seen a pocket watch; he had never seen a watch with hands. He thought that time could only be read digitally.

Mr O'Brien's eyes twinkled. 'Here, you hold it. In exactly three and a half minutes, Mr Moriarty will have found a solution.'

Tom took the watch and gazed, mesmerised, as the hand crept around the dial. Ten seconds, fifteen, twenty....

After precisely three minutes and thirty seconds, Mr Moriarty stretched his arms, unfolded his legs, leapt off his chair and smiled.

'We'll use the campanile bell.'

Tom looked puzzled.

'Tom,' said Mr O'Brien, 'when you entered the college, you must have noticed something in the middle of the square.'

Tom shut his eyes and tried to remember. 'Yes — yes, a belltower!'

'Well, that is known as the campanile. The bell is very old indeed, hundreds of years old, and it is only rung at exam-times and in cases of emergency.'

Mr Moriarty continued, 'Fortunately for us, the bell is now activated by electricity, so all we have to do is press a button.' He strode over to the door. 'There's a bell-button in each main room, so all we have to do is press the button and all hell — em, sorry — will break loose.' He rubbed his hands. 'It's known as "causing a diversion". While everyone is rushing into the square, you, Tom, can run to fetch Katie.'

Mr O'Brien patted Tom's head and said in a much more serious voice, 'Then we will go and visit the Book of Kells. You must see the Book of Kells before we can explain the code.'

∞

Katie shivered. She was cold and wet and very scared. What on earth had happened to Tom? Every few moments, she peered out from behind the pillar to see if there was any sign of him. Nothing. Every time she heard footsteps clattering on the cobblestones, she imagined a security guard coming for her.

She couldn't stay there much longer; she'd have to go and look for Tom. *I'll count to one hundred,* she decided, *and if he doesn't come back by then....* She shut her eyes and began to count.

She had got to seventy when she heard a loud clanging noise. It was so loud that she had to put her fingers to her ears to stop the vibration. What was it? Was it something to do with Tom?

Then there were shouts and the sound of people running. Katie curled herself into an even smaller ball. It was all over, they'd found Tom....

At that moment, she felt a tap on her shoulder.

'Katie, come on, get up! Listen, it's all right, it's for us; Mr O'Brien and Mr Moriarty have just caused a diversion. Come on, everyone's gone into the square. Quick, I'll take you back to the Long Room — that's where they are.'

Tom grabbed her by the hand and they went hurtling along the cobblestones, down the long corridor and through the great doorway into the Long Room, where the two men were waiting.

'Katie, delighted to see you. We've no time to lose. Quietly, now, just in case we bump into a guide.'

છ૭

They were standing beside an enormous table covered with glass. Under the glass was the most beautiful book Katie and Tom had ever seen. It lay open, so they could see the exquisitely ornamented letters in reds and yellows and greens; the ornamentation was made up of fantastic abstract animals and human forms.

'There, my dears.' Mr O'Brien was beaming proudly. 'As its keeper, I can tell you that this book — the Book of Kells — is Ireland's most treasured possession. It is over thirteen hundred years old, and we've had it here in Trinity College since 1661.'

Katie and Tom were transfixed. The swirls, the spirals, the patterns, all the animals.... Katie could make out a bird, a snake....

'You can see,' continued Mr O'Brien, 'that the decorations swamp the opening words, making them unintelligible, difficult to understand — at least, for anyone who does not already know what they should be.' He put a finger up to his chin. 'It has been suggested that this is deliberate, a sort of code.'

Mr O'Brien saw that Tom's eyes were bright with excitement. He continued, 'You see, we — Mr Moriarty and I, and the other guardians — are using a code based on these animals. I am telling you about it now because the holders of the code will be your contacts for the rest of the journey. We are all members of the Alphabet Network. This is why it is important for you to actually see the Book of Kells: so that you will understand.'

Katie was looking worried. 'I'm not very good at codes. I don't know if I'll be able to remember it.'

Tom punched her. 'Don't worry, I love working them out. Leave that to me!'

Mr O'Brien smiled. 'In fact, there is very little to work out. The code is based, very simply, on animals. You see, the Book of Kells has an animal alphabet: the monks decorated some of their letters with animals — fish, cats, birds, lions, snakes and dogs. So, for instance ...' He held up a drawing. 'What do you think this is?'

Katie put her head to one side. 'It looks like an R.'

Mr O'Brien nodded. 'Anything else?'

Tom shouted, 'A lion! It's a lion tangled around the R!'

'Well done, Tom! Now, as you proceed on your journey, your contacts will show you letters like this. You must only trust people who show you these letters — no one else. They themselves have animal code-names that correspond to the letters. Remember the note we deciphered?'

Tom nodded.

'I must warn you that there is no J and no K in this alphabet,' Mr O'Brien went on. 'The monks never used those letters. If anyone shows you a J or a K, it means that the code has been broken, or that this person is an outsider who has heard something about it.'

'Oh,' groaned Katie, 'I know I'm going to forget.'

'I've got an easy way of remembering,' suggested Tom brightly. 'K is for Katie, and J is for Jack. Remember Jack?'

'Good boy, Tom,' Mr O'Brien smiled. 'I think you'll have to be the carrier of the code. Now come on, you two, we're off to the circus!'

Chapter Six

Katie and Tom had never been to a circus, but they had heard their father talk about it — about the enormous circus that used to tour Ireland in the summertime. He had told them about the excitement in the town when the circus trucks and caravans moved in, and about the sight of the huge tent as it rose up into the sky; from miles away, you could see the big top with all its coloured flags flapping in the breeze.

Katie and Tom remembered these stories as they travelled out of Dublin in Mr O'Brien's car — as the keeper of the Book of Kells, he was allowed to own a car. They had to hide under a rug in the back until they got out of Dublin.

'Can't be too careful,' Mr Moriarty said.

Katie and Tom soon found out that there was a reason why they were going to the circus. Mr Moriarty's nephew was a clown, and he had agreed to let them join the circus!

'You see, my dears' — Mr O'Brien hadn't done much talking; he was too busy concentrating on his driving — 'it's an awfully good idea. The circus has just begun a tour of Ireland, so you'll be able to stay with them in complete safety until you reach your grandfather. I don't need to tell you that Mr Moriarty's nephew is a member of the Network; in the unlikely event that you have to leave before then, you'll be handed on to another friend who will help you. The main thing is that the circus will see you well away from Dublin.' He shivered. 'Very unsafe at the moment. They're strengthening their control in the towns and cities. The guides are everywhere, you see, because of the tourists; and the guides are their spies. Remember that, children: the guides are the enemy!'

'Who are "they", Mr O'Brien?' Katie asked. 'Are they child-stealers like the man in white?'

Mr O'Brien shook his head. 'Not exactly, my dears. Well, the man in white would belong to the organisation, and they do steal children. Their name is Tartarus. It's an old Greek word meaning "the darkness beneath the earth"; and that's exactly what they want to do — turn our beautiful country into a barren land....' His voice trailed off. 'Roadblock ahead! I think you'll have to get into the back, beside the spare tyre. Moriarty, help them.'

Quick as a flash, Mr Moriarty's long arms stretched into the back of the car and lifted the flap that covered the tyre. 'Sorry about this. In you get.'

Katie saw that some extra space — just enough to hide her and Tom — had been made beside the tyre.

'Don't worry,' whispered Mr Moriarty, as they climbed in. 'There are lots of air-holes; you won't suffocate.' And with that, he clamped down the flap and resumed his spider-like position.

'They must have heard already,' Mr O'Brien growled. 'God, they have spies everywhere!'

He pulled his car to a stop and rolled down the window. There were two guards at the roadblock; one of them stood by the window, while the other strolled around the little car.

'Problem?' Mr O'Brien smiled up at the guard.

'No, just our regular road check. Do you mind getting out for a minute?'

Mr O'Brien gritted his teeth. 'No, not at all.' He pointed to Mr Moriarty. 'Can you leave him where he is? He finds it very difficult to move.'

The guard smiled. 'Oh, that's all right — just want to check your mileage, lights, all that. Where are you off to, anyway?'

'We're actually going to the circus.'

'Bit old for that, aren't you?'

'Well, my friend's nephew belongs to it.'

'Oh, I see. Well, that's all right, then!'

Mr O'Brien was just about to hop back into the car when the guard added, 'You haven't by any chance seen two children, a boy and a girl?'

Mr O'Brien shut his eyes and pretended to think. 'Well, Guard, I've seen lots of children today, lots of boys and girls. What a strange question!'

The guard was becoming impatient. 'These two are different — thin, hungry-looking children. Anyway, there's a call out for them.' He shrugged. 'Must have run away. Okay, that's all — enjoy the circus!'

Mr O'Brien drove off as fast as he could. When they were well out of sight of the guard, he pulled the car over to the side of the road.

'Damn, Moriarty. Damn, damn! They're moving very quickly; looks like they're determined to stop the poor little beggars. You'll have to tell that nephew of yours to keep a right good eye on them. We'd better get them out from under that seat or they'll be goners!'

Mr Moriarty unfurled himself and lifted up the tyre-flap. 'Come on, children, out you get. We're on our way again. Problem over!'

'Big top coming up!' sang Mr O'Brien.

℣

Katie had never seen such an enormous tent. It was huge! There were the flags that her father had talked about. He hadn't told them about the smell — a sort of acrid, animal, yeasty smell. It wasn't unpleasant; in fact, she liked it. There was also a lot of noise in the air: horses whinnying, dogs barking, music coming in sporadic bursts, shrieking laughter — she'd never heard anything like it. The air was alive with sound. In England the air seemed dead; silent and dead.

She took Tom's hand. 'Tom, we're going to be happy here.'

Mr O'Brien threw his head back and laughed. 'Yes indeed, my dears; you're going to have to work at being happy. Didn't I tell you? You're going to be clowns, and here is your teacher!'

Katie and Tom couldn't see anyone, just two long sticks moving towards them. Their eyes moved upwards to an extremely tall man, a younger version of Mr Moriarty, perched on top of a pair of stilts.

'Are you coming down, Con?' Even Mr Moriarty had to crane his neck and shout.

The stilts wobbled for a moment. 'In a jiffy!'

Young Moriarty had long arms like his uncle, and in a second he had untied the stilt-straps and hopped down beside them. Katie was pleased to see that he had the same kindly expression as his uncle. She sighed. *No need to worry,* she thought; *he'll look after us until we get to Grandfather's.*

℣

That evening Katie and Tom felt that they had been magicked away to some far-off fairy place, where nothing was as it should be and all was illusion.

The circus ring became a kaleidoscope of colours: reds, blues, yellows, purples and greens. Katie's and Tom's ears were filled with the loud oompahs of bugles and trumpets, and their noses tickled with the heady mixture of sawdust and animal. It was truly magical, and, for two hours, Katie and Tom forgot their troubles.

They held their breath as the last acrobat climbed on top of the human pyramid, and Tom dug his nails into Katie's hand when the two trapeze artists met in the never-ending space above the ring. They roared with laughter when Young Moriarty appeared on his stilts with a tiny clown, holding an even tinier poodle, chasing after him.

'Well, my dears!' Mr O'Brien had enjoyed the circus just as much as they had. 'Wasn't that wonderful? And you're both going to be a part of it — see what fun you're going to have!'

'Can I be a clown? I want to be a clown!' Tom shouted.

Katie looked embarrassed. 'Mr O'Brien, sorry.... Tom, shh!'

The little man smiled. 'In fact, you're both going to be clowns. You'll be Young Moriarty's assistants. Katie, you look very tired. Are you all right, my dear?'

Katie shook her head, and Mr. O'Brien noticed that there were little worry-lines running across her forehead.

'Anything wrong, dear?'

'It's just that I don't think I'll be a very good clown. I mean, how do you be a clown? I know Tom'll be good at it, but who's ever heard of a girl clown?'

'Exactly!' Mr O'Brien took her arm. 'They're looking for a boy and a girl, so they won't think of clowns. Also, you don't have to tumble around the place; you can drive the little car. There's always one sad and serious clown that the others torment. Unfortunately, you'll have to get used to custard pies and drenchings!'

Tom was jumping up and down. 'I can't wait, I can't wait!'

Mr O'Brien put his arms around the children. 'Come on. I'm going to introduce you to Madame Bonbon. You're going to be staying with her; she's a fortune-teller, a sort of circus mother.'

Ȣ

Katie wasn't used to fat people. Everyone she had ever known had been thin. When she arrived in Dublin, she had thought that the people she saw were fat, when in fact they were simply well-fed. Nothing had prepared her for Madame Bonbon. She and Tom just stared and stared.

It was very rude to stare, but they couldn't help it. Madame Bonbon was enormous, and it wasn't as if she were particularly tall; she was just fat. She was dressed in a flowing purple dress that cascaded in ripples down to the floor. The hands that emerged from the sleeves were like bunches of plump white sausages, and the face that rose out of the robe was like a quivering pink jelly — a jelly with warm, liquid eyes, dark as raisins. There was a generous mouth with gleaming white teeth. As Madame Bonbon threw her arms around Mr O'Brien, he disappeared into her folds for a moment.

'Ah, *mon cheri*, 'ow are you? What are you bringing me?' She released Mr O'Brien, stood back and looked at Katie and Tom. Two large tears trickled down her quivering cheeks. '*Zut alors. Mon Dieu*, you poor leetle things — so thin, so *fatigués*!'

Suddenly she swooped down and drew them into her arms. Katie and Tom experienced a wonderful moment of purply, vanilla-scented warmth. There was safety under Madame Bonbon's heavy bosom.

'Don't worry, *mon ami*. I weel look after zem as if zey were my own. Now, off you go!'

She gently released Katie and Tom, and Mr O'Brien shook their hands.

'Goodbye. Don't worry — you'll be quite safe. Remember the animal alphabet, and in a few days' time you'll be reunited with your grandfather. Young Moriarty and Madame Bonbon will look after you until then. If by any chance anything should happen, there are friends in the country and they'll help you.'

Katie looked worried. 'Can't we just stay with the circus?'

'Of course, that is the plan. But Tartarus are desperate, and they have their spies everywhere. If they find out that you are with the circus, you must leave.'

'Why do they want us? Why are we so important?' asked Katie.

Mr O'Brien hugged her. 'You'll find out soon enough. For the time being, you just need to know as much as your father told you — the importance of the box — and nothing else.'

Chapter Seven

When Madame Bonbon led them to their new home, Katie and Tom soon forgot their sadness at Mr O'Brien's departure.

The outside of Madame Bonbon's caravan was painted in reds and yellows, with strange drawings of lions, fish and stars. 'The signs of the zodiac, *mes chers.*' Little curls of smoke were puffing out of the chimney on the caravan's roof. 'Queek, queek — I weel show you your beds and zen we weel eat. *Zut alors!* I weel 'ave to *feed* you!' She punched Tom's arm in disgust. 'Ah, bone, just bone.... In three days, Tom, you will be fat!'

She herded them up the steps, into the most mysterious and welcoming room that Katie had ever seen. In fact, it was a little like being enfolded in Madame Bonbon's bosom again. A warm golden glow came from four lamps which were attached to the walls; intricately patterned ruby-red rugs covered the floor, and velvet throws covered the beds; and at the end of the caravan, there was a little wood-burning stove surrounded by blue-and-white tiles.

Madame Bonbon could see into people's minds, and she saw the look in Tom's eyes. 'You like ... you like to play ze cards?'

'Oh yes, I love cards. I know all kinds of tricks!' Tom replied.

'But, Tom' — she put her finger to her lips — 'you must be careful. Zere is danger in ze cards.'

She saw that she had unsettled him. She hadn't meant to do that; it was just a feeling, after all....

'*Bon, mon cheri*, you can teach me some tricks. And I, *Tante* Bonbon, weel teach you some magic!' With one quick movement, she made three packs of cards appear in front of Tom. '*Voilà!* Now sit down here and practise. I weel prepare some food.'

While Katie and Tom sank into one of the sofas and played cards, Madame Bonbon busied herself at the stove. Occasionally there was a peal of song — 'De-de-de-tum....' — and wafts of delicious cooking-smells. Katie and Tom were at peace.

Soon Madame Bonbon produced the food: a plateful of hot bread covered in melting butter, and a chicken pie with a golden pastry crust. This was followed by glistening chocolate éclairs brimming with cream.

Tom groaned. 'I feel like bursting!'

Katie dabbed her lips politely. 'That was really delicious, Madame Bonbon. I've never tasted food like that before!' She shook her head at the memory of the little grey bits of food they had eaten in England.

'Oh, *mes pauvres*! While you stay with Madame Bonbon, you will grow. Now we clean up and you weel sleep. Tonight, while you sleep, the circus moves on!' She put a sausage-like finger to her nose. 'And, *mes enfants*, tomorrow you work. You weel learn 'ow to be clowns!'

ॐ

The next morning, after a large breakfast of eggs, sausages, tomatoes, rashers, thick slices of toast and hot chocolate, Katie and Tom went to their first lesson.

Young Moriarty was their teacher. 'Okay, kids, Clown Rule Number One: clowning is a very serious business, so don't make a joke of it! Ha, ha, ha.... No, seriously, you can't just go into the ring and fall around; there are certain movements.' And with that he turned a cartwheel.

Katie stared, open-mouthed. 'I couldn't possibly do that. I don't even know how to do a somersault!'

'Yes you do, Katie — just look,' said Tom, and proceeded to do two somersaults.

'Good boy, Tom. You're a natural!' Young Moriarty put his hand on Katie's shoulder. 'Now, Katie, it really is easy. Put your hands on the ground, then your head between your hands, and over you go.'

Katie closed her eyes and told herself, in her bossiest voice, *Now, Katie, if you really want to get safely to Grandfather, you have to become a clown. So just do a somersault.*

Gritting her teeth, she bent down and somersaulted.

'Bravo, Katie! You can do it!' Young Moriarty was clapping away. 'Tomorrow you'll have to learn how to cartwheel!'

∽

All that morning, Young Moriarty and Coco the clown taught Katie and Tom the basic rules of clowning. Young Moriarty was right: it was all more difficult and serious than it appeared.

'The main thing is for you to look like part of the troupe — not to look odd. That's in case there's anybody watching.'

Young Moriarty saw Katie's face go pale. He reassured her, 'I don't think there will be; but Tartarus's people seem to spring up from everywhere, and they know what you look like, so it's important that you fit in.'

Tom was jumping up and down in excitement. 'Oh, oh, Mr Moriarty, can I — can I squirt water?'

Young Moriarty looked at Coco, who was blowing his nose with a large red handkerchief. Everyone waited patiently for the foghorn noises to stop; then the handkerchief was removed from the nose, and a multicoloured rubber ball came flying over to Tom.

'Catch that,' boomed Coco, 'and the water gun is yours!'

Tom dived and caught the ball in his right hand.

'Well done, Tom — quick reaction! Yes, you can do the squirting. Perhaps we'll put Katie in the car,' pondered Coco. Katie's eyes lit up. 'Okay, I think we have a good pair of clowns here, Moriarty; pity we can't hold on to them for the season. Right, this afternoon there's a full dress rehearsal for tonight.'

৪১

That afternoon, Katie and Tom forgot all their troubles and worries. They couldn't remember ever having had such fun.

First of all, they had to have their make-up put on: white faces, red noses and wigs which felt like tight swimming-caps. They wore patchwork waistcoats and flapping trousers.

Katie's car had a loud hooter and windscreen wipers that sprayed water at anybody who came near. The exhaust made loud farting noises, and the whole thing was great fun. Young Moriarty and Coco threw custard pies at each other, and the rehearsal ended with Coco spraying the ring with a giant can full of shaving-cream.

Coco wiped his brow with his large red hankie. 'That's fine, and the juniors did very well. Thanks, everyone. Now we'll have a rest; the circus begins at eight p.m. sharp.'

When they got back to the caravan, Katie and Tom could smell something warm and buttery; Madame Bonbon was making pancakes. There were trickles of water running down her face, and the caravan was all steamed up.

'Ah, *mon Dieu, mes* clowns ... so 'ot! I thought I would make you pancakes, something light, *n'est-ce pas*? Ze pancakes, ze jam, ze bananas. Now a leetle rest before you eat, and zen you can tell me about ze rehearsal.'

After eating, Tom ran around outside with an imaginary water-gun. Katie helped Madame Bonbon with the washing-up.

'Oh, *Tante* Bonbon,' she said suddenly, 'I love it here. I'd love to stay in the circus forever!'

Madame Bonbon threw her arms around Katie. '*Cherie*, you would soon get tired of eet — ze always movement, always go, go, go, ze same people. *Non*, for you and Tom eet is good for a leetle while until you reach your grandpapa.' Her brow furrowed; she was about to say something else, but then she stopped. 'Now, *vite, vite*, get your brother. You 'ave to get ready; eet is nearly time, and Coco will be furious!'

∞

When Katie and Tom left for the big top, Madame Bonbon got up on a chair and took a large round object down from a shelf. The object was wrapped in a silk scarf. She put it on the table and carefully unwrapped it.

'Ah, my precious, maybe you weel tell....'

Madame Bonbon gazed into her crystal ball.

∞

The circus was packed; as usual, every single seat had a body sitting in it. Peeking from behind the curtain, Katie could see tier upon tier of faces, old, middle-aged, young. There were lots and lots of children — she'd never seen so many children before; it was as if all the children in the world had come into this great big tent. She could feel the excitement in the air.

Suddenly, a wave of shushing swept over all the talk and laughter. There was a general intake of breath, a waiting — and then there was Coco.

'Okay, clowns, at the ready. You're on first!' He tweaked Katie's cheek. 'Katie, don't look so worried. You're frowning. Clowns are supposed to be happy people! Relax — you and Tom were great this afternoon.'

At least Tom didn't have a care in the world. He was jumping up and down, waving his gun.

De-de-ta-ta-ta.... The music began, the talking stopped and they were on.

ॐ

Back in her caravan, Madame Bonbon was looking
into her crystal ball. What she saw didn't please her.
She hissed, '*Mon Dieu, zut alors!*' as she studied
what lay before her. Her pudgy hand went up to her
throat, and she angrily shook the ball. '*Non* — 'ow
could zey? Who told zem? Oh, *mes pauvres!*'

She felt for her chocolate box and hurriedly
munched the chocolates, one by one, until they
were all gone. Then she took her head in her hands
and cried. 'I want zem to stay.... Eet is too soon.
Maybe....'

She took one more look into the ball. '*Zut alors....*'
She shook it again and wrapped it up in its silk
scarf, then reached up and returned it to its shelf.

She dabbed her eyes and thought for a moment.
'Eet is necessary for me to tell Young Moriarty. He
weel know what to do.'

Chapter Eight

After the performance ended, to tumultuous rounds of applause, Katie and Tom went to have their make-up removed. Katie was surprised to see Madame Bonbon. She seemed to be looking for someone. Katie waved, and Madame Bonbon returned a sheepish half-smile.

Katie's heart lurched. Something had happened. Then she saw Young Moriarty bending down towards Madame Bonbon; there were head-shakings and more sheepish looks in Katie's direction.

She couldn't bear it any longer. She had to know. She slipped between the other clowns and made her way up to Young Moriarty and Madame Bonbon.

When Madame Bonbon saw her, she stopped in mid-sentence.

'*Zut alors*, Katie — your face, you 'aven't finished cleaning eet....'

Her voice trailed away as she saw the expression in Katie's eyes.

'Madame Bonbon, I know something is wrong, I know something's happened. It's about us, isn't it?'

Madame Bonbon looked at Young Moriarty, who shrugged and nodded. He knelt down and took Katie by her shoulders.

'Listen, Katie, we think your cover has been blown. We think Tartarus's people know where you are.'

Madame Bonbon's eyes were full of tears. 'You see, *ma cherie*, I 'ave ze crystal ball; I can look into ze future. Tonight, while you were performing, I took down ze stupeed ball, I looked into eet, and I saw danger. Nothink exact, but you and *le petit* Tom are in trouble.'

Young Moriarty turned to Madame Bonbon. 'Are you sure you didn't see anything else, anybody else? Think.'

Madame Bonbon shut her eyes. 'Let me see.... Zere was many, many black, brown and muddy colours — danger signs. Ah yes, one other theme: white — there was a man in a white suit....'

Katie screamed.

'*Ma cherie*, what did I say?'

Katie gasped, 'The man in the white suit ... he's been following us. He knows we're here.'

'Now look.' Young Moriarty grasped Katie's arm. 'Just because Madame Bonbon saw this fellow in her crystal ball, it doesn't mean that he knows you're here. It could just be a warning for the future that you're to look out for him. Anyway, the circus is moving tonight; and all the time we are moving closer to your grandfather.'

'But I didn't tell her,' cried Katie, fighting back tears. 'I didn't tell Madame Bonbon about him. How did she know? He must be near....'

A large purple handkerchief appeared in Katie's hand.

'*Cherie, cherie*, dry your tears. We'll go back to ze caravan for a good night's rest — and some 'ot chocolate.'

❧

The next day was going to be a scorcher — that was what Coco called it. When Katie and Tom woke up and went down the caravan steps, they saw that the circus was camped beside a river. A light mist lay over everything, and the grass was covered with tiny pearls of water. The air was warm, and Katie could hear birds tweeting high up in the sky. She looked up but couldn't see anything.

'Skylarks!'

The voice came from the other side of the caravan. Madame Bonbon was cooking breakfast.

'Breakfast outside today, *mes* clowns. Young Moriarty is joining us.'

Katie stretched. She'd forgotten about the night before, and now she felt content; it was all like a bad dream.

'And after breakfast, I theenk, a swim. Eat up! I wonder where Young Moriarty is — lazy man!'

Madame Bonbon was frowning as she and Katie washed up the dishes. 'Most unlike 'im.... Katie, take a leetle run and see where 'e is!'

Katie ran towards Young Moriarty's caravan. She felt a twinge of anxiety. *Ridiculous*, she said to herself; *he was only late for breakfast.*

When she reached his caravan, she noticed that only one of his stilts was outside. Her heart beat a little faster. She ran up the steps and rapped on the door. 'Mr Moriarty!'

'Come in!'

Her heartbeat returned to normal.

'It's only me — Katie. We were wondering —'

She peered around the door. Young Moriarty was lying on his bed, with an ankle the size of a football propped up on a cushion.

'Wow, what happened?'

Young Moriarty gave Katie a weak smile. 'Don't worry, it's not broken, just sprained. They always look worse than they really are. Now sit down and I'll tell you how stupid I've been. I got up really early this morning; thought I'd have a nice walk before Madame Bonbon's breakfast. I decided to walk on my stilts — a little practice. I had just gone a few paces when I heard a tearing sound and one of the stilts snapped under me — just like a matchstick.'

He shook his head. 'I can't understand it. First time it's happened. Anyway, it could be worse. I'll be right as rain in no time. I'll have to miss a couple of performances, of course, but there'll be no problem about getting a substitute stilt-man — they've done it before. Now, do you know what I'd really like? Some hot coffee and a sandwich made with the bacon that I didn't have!'

As Katie walked back to the caravan, the twinge of anxiety was still there. She knew that something wasn't right.

That night, before Tom and Katie went off to get ready for the circus, Madame Bonbon gave each of them an enormous hug. Tom felt so squeezed that he couldn't breathe. Katie let herself become entangled in Madame Bonbon's folds.

'Now, *mes enfants....*' Madame Bonbon dabbed her eyes. 'Off you go — even bettair than last night!'

After they had gone, Madame Bonbon looked up at the crystal ball wedged on the shelf. Should she — would she?

No, it had already told her enough: danger, there was danger about. Instead of sitting here staring into the wretched thing, she would have to do something about it. Those children had no one to look out for them, especially now that Young Moriarty was out of action. She, Madame Bonbon, would have to go to the circus ring herself.

She threw on her shawl. Was there anything else? Katie's box; she should really take that, just in case there was a break-in. She felt under Katie's mattress. There it was: an ordinary wooden box, very thin, about the size of a cigarette packet. She stuck it into her never-ending pocket and hurried towards the ring.

The tent was full, brimming over as usual, and thousands of pairs of eyes were staring in rapt attention as the trapeze artists effortlessly swung in the air and caught one another's wrists. Where were the clowns?

Madame Bonbon spotted them at the other side of the ring: Katie sitting in her little car, ready to go on, Tom doing some practice squirts with his gun. And that must be Young Moriarty's replacement. He was standing in the shadows, so she couldn't see him properly. The clowns would be on next; the audience always needed a lot of loosening up after the trapeze act. Madame Bonbon shivered. It was chilly, and she was pleased she had worn her shawl. She must remember to give the children extra-large mugs of hot chocolate tonight.

There was a collective sigh as the trapeze artists finished their most daring act, and then there was the music and the shuffling and the coughing and the tumult of applause. Madame Bonbon found herself clapping too.

'Magnifique, splendide! Bravo, bravo....'

The trapeze artists did happen to be French, and they did happen to be her nephews and nieces, so Madame Bonbon felt very proud. She kissed them as they came out of the ring, and then settled down to watch the clowns. After their act came the grand finale.

I'm getting good at this, thought Katie, as she manoeuvred the little car around the obstacles in the ring. Tom was enjoying himself immensely, leaning out of the side and squirting water at the audience, to shrieks of delight. Katie could see Madame Bonbon out of the corner of her eye. She thought of poor Young Moriarty with his sprained ankle: *He should be okay for tomorrow's performance....* As she thought of him, she looked for his replacement. He was at the far side of the ring.

'Tom, let's drive over to the stilt-man.'

Katie pressed her foot on the pedal, honked the horn and went flying over to the stilt-man. Just as Tom had his gun ready to squirt him, the stilt-man turned around and looked down at them.

Katie's heart did a somersault. Her hands slipped on the wheel. White trousers under the clown jacket. And the eyes behind the make-up — she'd recognise them anywhere.

Then it all became clear. Young Moriarty's accident had not been an accident.

The figure on the stilts threw his head back and laughed — a hollow laugh, an empty laugh that seemed to echo around the big top. It was as if the tent had suddenly emptied and there were only three people in it.

Katie pulled herself together and whispered to Tom, 'Tom, it's him — the man in the white suit. He can't do anything while the performance is on. We have to get help. I'm going to drive around to Madame Bonbon, and I want you to hop out and tell her. He must have friends here; they'll get us if we don't disappear.'

She waved up at the grinning face, then reversed the little car and drove back around the ring. When they got to Madame Bonbon, Tom hopped out. Katie could see him waving his arms and pointing at the stilt-man.

Round and round the ring again.... She could see the clowns getting ready to throw the custard pies; that meant they were nearing the end of the performance. Madame Bonbon and Young Moriarty didn't have much time.

Katie pushed her foot down on the pedal and went over to the clowns. She got out of the car and danced around, whispering instructions to them and generally pretending to be helpful. She could see the stilt-man out of the corner of her eye. He seemed to be getting impatient; he was signalling to someone in the audience. Katie gulped: *He mightn't even wait until the end of the performance....*

The custard pies were ready. The foam-squirters were ready. Katie watched as the clowns ran around the ring, custard pies in both hands; Tiny the midget clown ran after them, dragging the giant foam-squirter. The shrieks of the audience got louder; the clapping began, and the cries of 'Go on, go on!' Then Tiny was standing under the stilt-man, right between his legs, and — *poop! glop!* — a huge gush of foam shot up into the air and landed on the stilt-man's face.

The audience roared, the stilt-man roared. Tiny looked around, clapped his hands and gave the squirter another squeeze. This time the stilt-man tottered and fell.

Katie saw three men in shiny black raincoats leap over the barrier into the ring, but the custard-pie brigade were ready. *Splat, splat, splot* — three large yellow custard pies landed on the men's faces and trickled down their shiny raincoats.

The audience were howling with laughter, but Katie was worried. There were no more custard pies. Then she saw Madame Bonbon, Tom and Young Moriarty; he was waving his stick at Katie.

She hopped back into her car and raced towards them. She didn't dare look around, but she risked a peep. The stilt-man was getting up....

'Queek, queek, Katie!' Madame Bonbon was shouting. Katie could hear Young Moriarty calling to the trapeze artists, 'Go! Do what you can!'

And then she saw them leap onto their perches, high above the ring, and start to swing. The stilt-man was on his feet, stilts off. He began to march towards Katie, but one of the trapeze artists swung down with a hook in his hand and wrenched the stilt-man up into the air.

In the meantime, the tightrope walkers had thrown their rope across the ring and tripped up the three shiny raincoats. Tiny was there with his hose, covering them with a shower of foam.

'Time to go, Katie!' Young Moriarty was pulling at Katie's arm. 'We have to get out of here!'

Chapter Nine

Out into the night they went — Katie, Tom, Madame Bonbon and Young Moriarty. They rushed along under the light of the moon, full and white and benign.

'*Mes enfants*,' sobbed Madame Bonbon, '*mes enfants*, I could see — oh, I could see.... Oh, *mes pauvres*!'

'Where are we going?' asked Tom. He still didn't realise the seriousness of it, because it was all such fun.

'We're ... we're going ...' Young Moriarty was obviously still in a lot of pain. '... down to the river. We're going to get you in a boat.'

Katie kept looking back, imagining the white trousers flapping through the dark like sheets in the wind.

'Don't worry, my dear.' Madame Bonbon squeezed her hand. 'The circus people weel look after zem. Oh, I nearly forgot....' She dug her hand into her bottomless pocket. 'Your box; you şee, a leetle voice must 'ave told me you wanted eet tonight.'

She handed the box to Katie. Katie felt tears beginning to well up. *It isn't fair!* Why couldn't they just stay there and live in the circus forever? They didn't even know their grandfather. What was so important about that stupid little box, anyway?

She looked at Tom, Madame Bonbon and Young Moriarty. *It's for them, too; it's just as important for them.* She drew her shoulders back and marched forward behind Young Moriarty — down to the river, which shone like a ribbon of silver beneath the moon.

A boat was waiting. In the boat stood a figure in a hooded garment.

'Good, he's there.' Young Moriarty hobbled forward, took something from the figure and held it up. Katie saw that it was a metal disc on the end of a leather thong. The letter O was engraved on the disc, and the outline of an animal — it looked like an otter — was twined around it.

'Come on, quickly!' Young Moriarty was waving. 'Into the boat.'

He tugged Katie and Tom away from Madame Bonbon's arms. Madame Bonbon was sobbing inconsolably.

'Shh, Madame Bonbon,' whispered Young Moriarty. 'They'll hear you — sound travels!'

'Oh, *mes choux, au revoir, bonne chance....* I weel miss you!'

Then Katie and Tom were in the boat, and the hooded oarsman was pulling his oars in wide silver sweeps. Madame Bonbon and Young Moriarty got smaller and smaller as the boat drew downriver; soon they were just tiny figures on the riverbank, silhouetted against the moon. Katie hugged Tom as the figures finally disappeared from view.

It was cold on the river. 'I can see your teeth chattering, Tom.' She hugged him tighter.

The oarsman was silent, and even though Katie knew that they could trust him, because of the letter, there was still something spooky about him. In and out, the oars sliced through the water, leaving long silver trails in their wake. Occasionally a bird called, and once Katie thought she heard an owl — *to-whit, to-whoo*; otherwise there wasn't a sound. The animal world was asleep. Tom was also asleep, snoring gently against Katie's shoulder.

After a while, Katie noticed that the oars weren't dipping in and out quite as often as they had been. Then she saw that the oarsman had lifted them out of the water and that they were gliding under a canopy of trees. He brought the boat to a stop and steadied it against the bank.

Then he turned around. Katie saw that he was dressed in a brown robe made out of a thick wool-like material. He threw his hood back, and Katie saw a handsome young man with twinkling eyes. He put out his hand.

'I'm Brother John, code-name Otter. I'm sorry I didn't introduce myself before, but I wanted to get us away as quickly as possible.'

Katie was still staring at him in a puzzled way.

'Oh, you're worried about the dress? Well, you don't look so normal yourself!'

Katie remembered that she and Tom were still dressed in their clown outfits.

'A right funny lot we are. Have you never seen one of these habits before?'

Katie shook her head.

'I'm a monk. Of course, you're from England — there wouldn't be any monks over there. Well, you'll see plenty in Ireland! Now, I don't know your full story, but I've been told that you're very important. You're going to your grandfather's, right?'

Katie nodded.

'Well, we're going to hide you in our monastery for a few days, until they call off the search.'

Katie took a deep breath. 'But why, Brother John? Why are they so desperate to find us?'

'If I knew, I'd tell you. All I know is that it isn't every day the old Alphabet Network is reanimated; it must be something serious. Now we'd better get going again. The monastery is only about an hour from here.'

Just as Brother John was getting the oars in place, Katie heard a noise. It was a kind of background noise — a rumbling sound, like clouds knocking together, a long way off, before a thunderstorm. But the sky was clear, full of stars, and there were no clouds.

'Brother John, listen....'

The monk laid down the oars and cocked his head.

'Whatever it is, it's coming closer; and it's certainly not thunder, I can tell you that. Quickly, the two of you, lie down flat in the boat. I'm going to drag it right against the bank, under those trees. It must have been God himself who guided us to this place. Now, shh.'

The noise was coming closer, and it had turned into a *clackety-clack-clackety-clack* — a helicopter. Tom woke with a start.

'They're really out in force,' whispered Brother John. 'Down — down! Those machines are vicious; they could spot a squirrel with the lights they've got.'

The helicopter was right over them and the noise was deafening. A bright white light lit up the whole riverbank, and Katie could hear animals scattering into the bushes.

'Don't move an inch,' whispered Brother John. 'They can detect the slightest movement.'

It seemed as if the helicopter was directly on top of them, and Katie imagined the man in the white suit pointing down — *There they are, got them, like rats in a trap....*

For one awful moment, the light shone down through the tree canopy, and the three froze. Katie was even thinking of throwing the wretched box into the river — at least they wouldn't get their hands on that!

And then, just as suddenly as it had appeared, the light disappeared. The helicopter drew away and the horrible clacking sound faded into the distance.

Tom started to get up, but Brother John put a large hand on his head and shoved him down.

'Patience. You don't know their tricks. Just wait and listen for the silence again.'

The silence returned and Brother John resumed rowing, and in the lightening sky they arrived at a lake. In the middle of the lake was an island, and on the island was the monastery.

Chapter Ten

'Hey, that's *old*!'

They were walking up the path from the pier towards the monastery.

'Tom, don't be so rude!' Katie punched him on the arm.

Brother John laughed. 'Katie, don't be so hard on your young brother. He's quite right: the monastery is very old. Parts of it go back to the twelfth century, almost a thousand years ago; but, as you'll soon see, it's full of life.'

As they got closer to the monastery, Katie understood what he meant. The air around the monastery seemed to vibrate: bees zoomed here and there; butterflies — blue, orange and multicoloured — glided about, and one or two of them gently brushed Katie's cheeks with their wings. The monastery lay in a pool of green, a meadow where poppies, daisies, buttercups and wild roses grew in profusion.

Katie stood on the path and stared at the long, waving grasses and flowers. Brother John gently took her by the arm; he named the flowers and explained why there were so many butterflies and bees. Tom had gone running through the grass, zigzagging and making aeroplane noises, finally collapsing into a heap in the middle of the sweet-smelling grass.

Brother John shook his head in wonderment. 'Of course, you two have never seen grass, flowers, insects, butterflies — all the things we take for granted.'

When Brother John took them into the monastery, Katie had difficulty seeing; the sudden darkness made her feel as if she had gone blind. Her ears were all right: she could hear the most beautiful chant, many men singing as if with one voice, clear and melodious, unaccompanied, echoing off the walls of the monastery. In a strange way, the beauty of the music made her gulp back tears. She felt happy and safe again. This was a good place.

As if he could read her thoughts, Brother John said, 'You'll be safe here. This monastery is actually the headquarters of the Alphabet Network. Now come on; I'll show you where you're going to sleep.'

Katie and Tom followed the monk down stone-flagged corridors. Katie was able to see again, but there wasn't much light, and what there was streamed through narrow little windows set deep in the walls.

Slap, slap, went the monk's sandals. 'Here we are. Pretty simple, but you'll be warm and comfortable enough. It won't be for long; we'll have you off on the next stage of your journey in a few days' time.'

When Brother John had left them, Tom wrinkled his nose. 'Katie, I don't really like it here; it's too quiet. I want to go back to the circus. I loved Madame Bonbon.'

Katie hugged him. 'Oh, Tommy, I know — it was like we were part of a family. I always knew you were a bit of a clown!'

Tom punched her.

'No, seriously; you're good at tricks and that sort of thing. Maybe when this is all over and we get this box to Grandfather, he might — he might just let us —'

Brother John's head popped around the door. 'Come on, you two, supper. You must be starving.'

'Katie!' Tom tugged at her sleeve. 'Let us what, Katie?'

But Katie was smoothing her hair and getting back into her bossy-sister mode. 'Can't remember. Come on. We're guests, we can't be late.'

The refectory was huge, and, except for the long table and benches, completely bare. There was an enormous cross on the wall facing the door, and the other walls were covered with banners hanging down to the floor. Each banner bore a picture of an elaborately drawn animal.

'The animal alphabet,' breathed Katie.

Brother John nodded. 'I thought you'd notice. Remember what I told you: this is the centre.'

Katie and Tom were hungry, and they dug into the platefuls of crusty bread covered with yellow butter and creamy cheese. There were jugfuls of milk and bowls of apples, pears and plums — a feast. None of the other monks paid much attention to Katie and Tom — none, that is, except one very large monk who sat at the end of the top table. Katie could see that he was observing them.

She nudged Brother John. 'Who's that very big monk at the end of the table?'

Brother John smiled. 'He's our Father, our Abbot. I'm glad you asked, because he wants to meet you after supper. He feels that you're owed an explanation. A lot has happened to you since you arrived in Ireland, and you don't really know why.'

☙

Later that evening, while Tom was helping Brother John with the cows, the Abbot took Katie for a walk in the monastery gardens. As they walked, he told them the names of the different flowers that they passed, names that rang in Katie's head like a song: lady's tresses, cuckoo flower, eyebright, bird's-foot trefoil....

'And that's a foxglove.' The Abbot pointed at a tall blue flower. 'It contains a very powerful medicine which we use in our infirmary. In fact, most of these flowers contain remedies for something — you see how good Nature is. These plants and flowers have been growing here for centuries, and Mother Nature is happy that we should use them, as long as we don't interfere with her. Mother Nature does not like interference.'

'Is that what's happened in Britain and Europe?'

'Yes, my dear, exactly. Gross interference, getting worse and worse all through the last century.' The Abbot bent down and plucked a blue flower. 'Smell this.... And so the catastrophes began to happen: dried uplands, infertile animals, and infertile people. Nature had had enough.'

'But how did Ireland escape?'

'Ah, there again we have to return to the end of the last century, when we had years and years of the most awful summers — rain, rain and more rain. It had something to do with a phenomenon called "El Niño", which upset the normal jet stream and currents and brought a sort of permanent cloud mass to the Atlantic. Ireland was right in the middle of it. It was very depressing at the time; I remember my grandparents moaning and groaning, "Look at the boiling weather they're having over in England. Isn't it well for them!" But, of course, that was before anyone knew what the boiling weather would do.'

The Abbot sighed. 'Thank God we did have the cloud, and thank God we never went along with that genetic interference with animals and vegetables. And so, you see....' He stopped suddenly, and, drawing his arms back, he embraced the trees, practically translucent in their greenness; the blues, whites, reds and yellows of the flowers; the constant insect activity, bees collecting pollen, butterflies alighting on flowers; and the ever-present scent, a mixture of sweetness and grass. Katie closed her eyes and breathed it all in.

Then she felt the Abbot clutching her arm. 'Katie....' He was staring into her face. 'Katie, that is why you and Tom are so important, why what's in that box is so valuable, why we've revived the Alphabet Network: because we're in danger of losing it all, all this....'

His voice broke. 'Greed did it before, as I told you, and greed is going to do it again, here in Ireland. Have you ever heard of Togo Yukinora? He's the head of one of the most powerful and destructive corporations in the world. Thank God, the government of Ireland has always had the honesty and wisdom to refuse his offers — up to now, that is....'

'What's my grandfather got to do with all this?'

The Abbot gazed up at the sky. 'Well, Katie, back in the last century — at the time I was telling you about — there were groups of young people called eco-warriors who tried very hard to stop the damage that was being done to the environment. The Alphabet Network was set up as a means of communication between the groups.'

'Was my grandfather an eco-warrior?'

'He was indeed, Katie; and he went on to become

Minister for the Environment. Then he found out that one of his colleagues, another minister, was making secret deals that nibbled into our natural resources. Your grandfather went to the First Minister with his suspicions, and the First Minister believed him — he and your grandfather were good friends — but he couldn't do anything, because your grandfather had no proof. And then, of course, the other minister forced your grandfather to resign.'

Katie looked up into the Abbot's face. 'But why is he in hiding?'

'Because there were death threats, Katie, and an assassination attempt. Tartarus are still afraid of him. He's the only man who has the power to stop them — if he could get the evidence....'

Katie shivered.

'Are you all right, my dear? I didn't mean —'

'No, no....' whispered Katie, as visions of the man in the white suit flashed through her mind. She had a sudden awful flash of Tom — Tom hurt, Tom on his own, calling for her.... 'No, I'm fine, Father Abbot. It's just got a little chilly. I'd like to go back inside now. I want to see Tom.'

Chapter Eleven

After supper one night, almost a week later, the Abbot called Katie and Tom over to him.

'My dears, we've received a message.'

'Is it in code?' asked Tom, his eyes gleaming.

The Abbot nodded. 'Here, have a look. Do you think you could decipher it?'

Tom looked at the piece of paper. 'Yes, Mr O'Brien showed me how. Well, it's to Fish....'

The Abbot smiled. 'That's my code-name. Go on.'

UIFZ IBWF DBMMFE PGG UIF TFBSDI QSPDFFE UP SPPTLZ

The Abbot and Katie stood by as Tom, pencil in hand, tongue sticking out, decoded the message.

'There.' He held out the piece of paper.

'"They have called off the search. Proceed to Roosky." And it's from Eagle. Well,' said the Abbot, 'we were very pleased to have you for a little longer than planned....' He saw that Tom had grown at least an inch in that week, and that Katie's cheeks had filled out. They were both healthy and brown — nothing like the miserable children who had first arrived at his monastery.

He continued, 'But, as you see, the time has come.'

He saw disappointment come into Tom's eyes, and fear into Katie's. Tom was the first to speak. 'I don't want to go. I love it here!'

Katie put a hand on Tom's arm. 'Tom, we have to go. I'm sure we can come back on a visit.'

The Abbot smiled at Katie, and his smile said, *I know you're afraid, but I also know that you are strong and that we can depend on you.*

Then he spoke in a very serious voice. 'There are signs that Tartarus are becoming more powerful, that we are being overcome; it won't take long for the balance to tip completely. So, my dears ...' He hugged them both. 'Brother John is going to take you across to the town, and there you'll meet another Network member. Now, off with you and have a good sleep; but I'll give you my blessing first.'

Putting his hands on their heads, he intoned, 'May God bless you and keep you, and may you reach your grandfather in safety, for we all depend on you.'

❧

The next day, as they glided across the lake in the early-morning mist, Katie could hear the monks' chants rising into the air and following them. She snuggled up to Tom — on their way again. Brother John was quiet, except for a few words now and then: 'I'll miss you. You will come back, now won't you?'

∞

Roosky was really more like a village than a town, with just one main street, but even at this early hour it seemed quite busy. There were groups of people sitting outside cafés beside the pier. 'Tourists,' muttered Brother John. 'They're everywhere.'

Katie and Tom looked hungrily at the plates of brown bread, muffins and buns that sat on the cafés' tables. They hadn't had time to have breakfast before they left. Tom could feel his stomach rumbling. He tugged at Brother John's arm. 'Brother John, can we have breakfast? I'm starving!'

The monk looked anxious. 'No, Tom, not yet. I have to hand you over — I'm sure you'll get something to eat then. Listen, Tom, just be quiet and patient; I'm not used to these secret shenanigans.'

Minutes passed, and Katie knew that the monk was becoming more anxious and impatient. He twisted his rope belt round and round his hand. Tom had run off to a nearby tree and was perched on a branch like a bird, watching every morsel that the tourists put into their mouths.

Katie was getting worried. What if something had happened? What if they had been found out — what if the contact had been captured? At least they were with Brother John....

She was just beginning to feel quite happy at the idea of returning to the island when she saw a slim, tallish woman striding towards them. The woman's long blond hair was tied up in a plait, which lay on top of her head in a sort of bun. Her gold hoop earrings glinted in the sun, and as she came closer,

Katie noticed that many of the tourists had stopped eating to watch her. There was something attractive, star-like, about her — a sort of shining.

As the woman held out her hands, Katie saw that her smile was warm. She couldn't see her eyes, because they were hidden behind dark glasses.

'Well, good morning to you!' As she held out her right hand to Brother John, Katie saw that there was a ring on the little finger; the woman held the finger up, and Katie saw that it was a signet ring with the initial in the form of an animal. Brother John quickly glanced at the ring and nodded. He seemed very relieved.

The woman bent down and held out her hand to Katie. 'My name is Stella Craven. And you are...?'

'Katie.' Katie wished Miss Craven would take off her glasses; she always felt uneasy if she couldn't see people's eyes.

Miss Craven straightened up and frowned. 'But there should be another.'

Brother John looked around. 'Oh, he's around. You know what boys are like — he'll be up a tree somewhere.'

Miss Craven relaxed. 'Fine. Well, we'd better be off.' She smiled at Katie. 'We're going to be very busy today! Thank you, Brother, for bringing them over.'

Brother John nodded and turned to Katie, and she hugged him tightly. 'Look after yourself now, Katie, and that brother of yours.'

Tom had reappeared, and he leapt on Brother John's back, his arms thrown around the monk's neck. 'Don't go, don't go! Come with us! Can't you come? Please!' Did Katie imagine it, or did she see a tremor of alarm twitch in Miss Craven's cheek?

'No, no, Tom, I have to get back. Now you be a

strong fellow, keep an eye on Katie — go on with you.' Brother John gently released himself from Tom's arms, waved goodbye and was off.

Miss Craven stood between Katie and Tom, her hands resting lightly on their shoulders. Her bright-red nails were very long, and Katie wished that they didn't dig into her shoulders.

The boat was soon out of sight. Tom groaned, 'Can we please have something to eat? I'm so hungry!'

Miss Craven patted his hand. 'Of course, my darling. There's a little café beside my shop, so while I gather up some things, you two can have breakfast — how about that?'

Katie and Tom nodded. Katie was beginning to feel better. Miss Craven did seem all right, and she was part of the Network: she had shown Brother John the code. But Katie still had a little niggling feeling in her stomach.... Maybe it was hunger.

⁌

An hour later, after two boiled eggs, three slices of toast and honey, a banana, and a large cup of tea, Katie could still feel the niggle in her stomach.

Katie and Tom were sitting in Miss Craven's shop while she bustled about. Miss Craven owned a wool shop. Balls of wool lay around everywhere, samples of sleeves were draped on hangers, and there was even a ram's skull with two curled horns on the wall.

Tom kept wrinkling his nose, and every now and then he would sneeze. 'My nose is tickling, Katie. I don't like it here, I don't like the smell.'

Katie sniffed. He was right: even though her nose wasn't that sensitive, the air seemed musty and peculiar. The niggle got bigger. She wished she could see Miss Craven's ring, see it for herself. She tried to remember what Brother John had said while they were rowing across to the town. *How much does he know? How well does he know the code? Why did he keep saying he knew nothing about secrets?*

She shook her shoulders. She had to stop this; she was analysing too much. Miss Craven did seem all right: she was kind and warm, she called them 'darling', she owned a wool shop....

Katie closed her eyes, and images of fluffy white sheep danced up and down in her mind. Then the sheep turned into fluffy white clouds, and suddenly an enormous ram with red eyes stuck his head through the clouds and snarled....

Katie felt a hand on her shoulder.

'Katie, darling, are you all right? You look like you've seen a ghost.' Miss Craven's plait shook from side to side. 'We're going to get you busy now — no time for dreaming! Can you help me carry this wool out to the van?'

Katie was a little surprised that Miss Craven had a van, but she was also relieved. It was nice to know that they had someone powerful on their side.

'Where are we going?' asked Tom.

'To Breffni Castle, so I can sell my wool to the tourists there. Have you ever been to a castle before?'

'No!' cried Tom. 'Will there be dungeons and slit windows for firing arrows?'

'Oh yes,' smiled Miss Craven. 'Now come and help me carry these boxes, or you might end up in a dungeon!'

❧

The castle wasn't far from the town, but when it appeared, it was totally unexpected. They rounded a corner on the narrow country road, and there was the grey stone castle with its two turrets, on the edge of a lake. There was a lot of activity outside it; Katie saw at least three tourist buses, a large black minibus with tinted windows, and groups of people being led by green-uniformed guards. She shivered.

'Anything wrong, dear?' Miss Craven put her red-nailed hand on Katie's knee. 'I don't think you're well. Are you coming down with something?'

'No, no, it's all right — I'll be fine. Is the castle always this busy?'

'Well, Katie, tourism is our main industry — Séamus Slevin, the Minister for Tourism, has done wonders. But we also hold conferences at the castle. Today there's a conference on water purification or something boring like that. Now come on, let's get inside or we'll lose business.'

Katie's niggling feeling had returned. Had it ever gone away? Was it the sight of the green-suited guides, or was it the sinister-looking man standing beside the minibus? There was nothing for it: she would have to see that ring for herself....

'Katie, what are you doing? My goodness, you are a dreamer! Come on, bring in the last box!'

∞

Later, while Miss Craven was selling her wool, Katie dragged Tom into a corner.

'Tom, we're in a trap. Shh, don't say anything! I can't prove it yet, but I'm sure Miss Craven isn't really part of the Network. I know something's wrong. I want you to start doing your card tricks, and when she isn't busy, get her to join in. You know that trick you do where the person hides a card under her hand?'

Tom nodded. 'Yes, and I have to try and guess the card. That's one of my best tricks.'

'Well, I want you to play it with her. Study her hands, like you're trying to see the card. Really, of course, what you have to do is study her signet ring, the one with the code.'

Chapter Twelve

That evening, the tourists had all gone and the castle was quiet — eerily quiet. Miss Craven was stretching and yawning: 'Oh — hmm....' She reminded Katie of a cat, especially when she swished that plait of hers and narrowed her eyes.

The more Katie observed Miss Craven, the more her suspicions hardened. It was strange that she had made no mention of their future plans and asked no questions about their past.

Miss Craven lit a cigarette, and the smoke curled up, making her green eyes milky and strange. 'Darlings, I don't know whether I told you or not, but we're spending the night here in the castle. Have you ever stayed in a castle before?'

Katie and Tom shook their heads.

'Oh, it will be exciting, then! You see, with busloads of tourists due in tomorrow and this conference tonight, it would be far too....' Her voice trailed off and she smiled at them. Katie noticed that her eyes weren't smiling; they were like two blocks of green ice. 'So beddy-byes for you two in the turret of the birds.' She stretched again, and gave the closest sound to a purr that a human could make.

Maybe I'm imagining it, thought Katie; *maybe I'm just comparing her to Madame Bonbon.* This woman was nothing like Madame Bonbon.

Katie kicked Tom and made a card-playing motion with her hand. Tom winked back at her and took out his pack of cards. 'How about a game, Katie?'

'Okay, let's play Snap.'

They played several games of Snap; with each game, they got louder and louder.

'Children, can you be a little quieter? Play something else!' Miss Craven's voice had an edge to it.

Tom grinned at Katie. 'Card tricks, then!'

No matter how many times Katie saw Tom do his card tricks, she never lost her wonder. How did he do them? And how was he going to play the most dangerous game that he had ever played?

Katie pointed to Miss Craven.

'Miss Craven?' Tom used his sweetest voice.

Miss Craven blinked.

'Would you like to see some of my card tricks?'

Her eyes stared for a moment, and then she smiled. 'Why, yes, Tom. Show me how good you are.'

Katie watched while Tom went through his best tricks. Miss Craven was genuinely impressed, but Katie saw that she was beginning to get fidgety.

'Tom, do one more — do the hand-over-card trick, you know the one.'

Tom nodded and held out the pack to Miss Craven. 'Okay, take a card — any card. I'll turn around and shut my eyes so I can't possibly see. Now put the card under one of your hands, and tell me when you're ready.'

'Ready!' Miss Craven had her two hands flat on the table. *So far so good,* thought Katie.

Tom turned around and opened his eyes, and Katie's heart pounded as he went through the motions of searching for the card. He bent down and inspected Miss Craven's two hands. The long, red-painted nails didn't budge.

Imagine if she suspects anything.... Maybe there's nothing to suspect; maybe she really is a member of the Network.... Katie shut her eyes and thought a prayer, a prayer that she and Tom were in safe hands.

Tom was examining the ring hand. 'Come on, Tom.' Miss Craven was becoming impatient. 'I'll accuse you of cheating in a moment!'

'Finished!' Tom returned to his chair and shuffled through the pack of cards. Katie tried to read his face, but Tom, as a good card-player, was an expert at not letting his feelings show.

'Miss Craven, you have — ta-da! — a queen of spades! And that card is under your left hand!'

Miss Craven threw back her head and laughed. 'Wonderful, Tom — oh, wonderful! Hmm....' She paused for a moment. 'Perhaps I'll get you to do some after-dinner tricks for our delegates tonight! Speaking of which, I must go and see to the kitchens. You two stay here. I can see that the cards will keep you amused!'

She swept out of the room, glancing back and waving as she went.

Katie let her breath out. 'She really is nice.... But why's she talking about the delegates? What's her wool shop got to do with delegates?'

Tom was carefully putting the cards back into their packet. He held up the last card, a jack. 'There's your answer.'

'A jack?'

'Remember: K for Katie, J for Jack — remember that little boy we met? The letter was a J.'

Katie put her hands over her eyes. It was all right

to have niggles and doubts, but now to have them actually confirmed.... Tartarus obviously didn't know about the two missing letters, but they'd heard of the code, the animal alphabet.

'We're sitting in their trap. What are we going to do? What are they going to do with us?'

'You have to think of a plan, like you always do.'

Katie glared at him. 'Why is it always me? — We're on our own now, Tom; it's like at the beginning, before we met Mr Moriarty and Mr O'Brien. I feel so lost.'

Tom came over and threw his arm around her. 'Oh, Katie, you always get us out of trouble. I feel safe with you. We'll have to escape!'

'But how?'

'We can go now, slip out while she's away.'

'No, she could come back any minute....' Katie took a few deep breaths and felt more in control again. 'No, we'll wait until tonight. Remember, she said she was going to be busy with the conference? We'll slip out then. It's important that we don't give anything away, don't make her suspicious. She thinks we trust her, so we'll go on pretending; and then tonight, after we've gone to bed, we'll escape.'

ॐ

That night, Katie and Tom meekly agreed to Miss Craven's suggestion of early bed. She seemed to have forgotten her idea of having Tom do card tricks for the delegates. She showed them to a tiny room in the bird turret, at the top of about a hundred winding stairs. It was going to be a very cold night.

'Thank goodness we won't be spending the whole

night here,' Katie whispered. 'It's horrible. And now I know why it's called the bird turret; look out there.'

Tom stood on tiptoe and looked out of the narrow window. Thirty pairs of yellow eyes stared back at him. He screamed, 'What are they?'

'Crows, I think.'

'Crows as old as time.' Miss Craven had reappeared with blankets and pillows. 'Well, certainly as old as the castle. They're meant to guard it. There's a story that hundreds of years ago, when this castle was first built, it came under attack — a surprise attack — and the thirty sentries were killed. They say that the spirits of the sentries live on in the crows. They'll defend the castle against anything.' She smiled. 'Don't worry, children, they won't do you any harm, especially when they see you with me. I feed them the odd mouse or two, so they regard me with special affection.'

She tossed back her head and laughed. 'Anyway, have a good night. I have to see to my delegates.' Then she was off, blowing them a kiss.

'Are you sure, Katie?' Tom whispered.

'Sure about what?'

'Sure that she's one of them. It's just that —'

'Listen, Tom, it's just that she's in good form tonight because she's got us — got us in her trap. She's going to hand us over, put us in a cage....' Katie shivered. 'She's probably going to come and get us out of our beds tonight. Besides, the most horrible people inside can be the nicest outside, so don't be taken in by her. Let's get into bed and pretend to be asleep, just in case she comes back to check.'

Sure enough, after about half an hour, Katie heard a soft thud on the stairs; then the door rattled slightly, as if someone was leaning against it. Katie breathed heavily and pushed her way down under the blankets. She hoped that Tom was under his and not squirming around.

After a minute or two, Katie heard the thuds again as the watcher's footsteps receded down the stairs.

'Tom,' she whispered, 'Tom.' *He's probably really gone to sleep*, she thought. 'Tom?'

'Mmm....'

'Tom, it's time to go. Come on.'

'Ugh — do we have to? I'm lovely and warm now. Can't we stay till tomorrow and escape then?'

'Don't be so stupid! Now's our only chance. They're planning to catch us tonight; tomorrow we'll be on our way back to Dublin in that black minibus!'

Holding hands, they tiptoed out of the room and crept down the stairs. Luckily there were no lights on anywhere, so it was quite dark.

As they came to the end of the stairway, they heard a sound — a sort of muffled roaring. Katie stopped. *The delegates!* She closed her eyes and imagined a roaring beast waiting to pounce.

At the bottom of the stairway there were two passages, one leading to the main castle door, the other to the conference hall. Tom was already tugging at Katie's hand, pulling her in the direction of the door. She bit her lip and then made a decision: she pointed in the other direction — the direction of the roaring.

Tom's eyes widened.

'I know we should get out as fast as we can, but I really want to see what's happening. It might be useful later on. Let's just go and have a look. This passage actually leads to a gallery over the conference hall — I found it this afternoon — so we can look down from there.'

Holding hands, they tiptoed along the passage, staying close to the wall. The roar got louder and louder, and Katie was sure she heard clapping. Then they were in the gallery, looking down on a hall full of people — mostly men, but there were a number of women.

There was a long table on a sort of platform, and a giant screen filled the wall behind it. Katie froze as she saw her own face and Tom's, ten times enlarged, smiling down at the delegates. She quickly put her hand over Tom's mouth before he saw it and yelped.

Three people were sitting at the table: Miss Craven, beaming at the delegates; beside her, a small, fat, bald-headed man in black, a tiny pair of glasses perched on his nose; and next to him — Katie stifled a groan. The man in white!

She clutched Tom. 'Oh, Tom, I can't believe — it's no use — we'll never escape....'

Tom squeezed her hand. 'We've done all right so far. They think we're in bed. We're one step ahead of them: they don't know we know.'

Katie pulled herself together. 'Shh — listen.'

The small fat man was speaking. 'And so, dear friends, our plans are nearly completed. Next week we sign our agreement with the Yukinora Agro-Indian Corporation, who will pay us an enormous price for our water.' He smiled at the delegates, his glasses glittering in the light. 'Nothing can stop us now. As you know, Miss Craven has rounded up' — he turned around to the huge photograph of Katie and Tom — 'our two little friends. We'll search them tonight — wake them up when they're too cold and frightened to give us any trouble. We're sure they've got what we want. Then they'll be on their way back to England. I've been on the phone to a friend in desperate need of labour; something to do with a shortage of little fingers — ha, ha, ha....'

Katie had stiffened. She'd heard that voice before, somewhere. She shut her eyes. *If he keeps talking —*

But then the whole hall resounded to the laughter and clapping of the delegates. Tom buried his head in Katie's chest and sobbed. 'Katie ... Katie ... back to England.... Stop them, Katie.... Find a way....'

The speech had made Katie angry. *How dare he! Well, at least they're wrong about one thing: they haven't got us.*

'Come on, back the way we came.' She crept back down the passage. 'Okay, Tom, all clear!'

She felt the back of her neck prickling just before she heard the cry. She spun round, and there was Tom, struggling in the arms of one of the guides.

He looked terrified, but he managed to shout out, 'Go, Katie! Go!'

Katie hesitated. Then she ran, ran as fast as her legs would carry her — two steps, three steps at a time — down the stairs. She could hear Tom's shouts echoing behind her: '... leave ... don't leave....' The words were indistinct, but she thought that was what they said, and her heart felt as though it was cracking in two. Still she ran. She wouldn't think of Tom, brave Tom. Tears ran down her cheeks — she'd get away, she'd come back to save Tom....

She heard the clatter of other feet on the stairs. *Which way?* There was a faint light on the left — *It must be that way!* She raced as she'd never raced before, her long legs sprinting along — *Don't think, just run* — and there was the door. Shut ... it couldn't be locked!

The footsteps were getting louder, there were more of them now. Katie put her two hands on the massive handle and wrenched it.

The door creaked open and she was out — outside the castle. *Don't stop, don't look back....* Her chest was heaving. On and on — she could hear shouts behind her — across the car park, onto the road....

She felt safer now. There would be people on the road; they'd help her, they'd come back with her to get Tom.

But the road was empty, a line of white curling off into the distance. The castle was all lit up now, and there were figures running everywhere. It was no use.

She stopped, bent down and tried to catch her breath. Out of the corner of her eye she saw something scamper into a hedge. She clenched her teeth. *Don't give up now.*

Katie stepped onto the verge beside the hedge and got down on her knees. Sure enough, there was a sort of passageway through the hedge. She crawled in and saw that it led to a flattened hollow. She sniffed: there was a curious smell, earthy and sweet, not unpleasant; an animal smell. This must be an animal's nest — quite a large animal, bigger than a squirrel. Katie took a deep breath and told herself that it didn't matter, it wouldn't harm her. She sat in the hollow and hugged her legs.

The voices were getting closer; feet were tapping along the road. She thought she heard Miss Craven's voice. Then the tapping feet stopped right beside the hedge, and Katie knew it was Miss Craven when she heard her shriek, 'Katie! I know you're there! You can't have gone far. We've got dear little Tom in our dungeon, and if you don't come out, *I'll* be playing some tricks on *him*!'

Katie put her hands over her ears and buried her head between her knees. She mustn't listen, couldn't listen. She blocked everything out of her head and hoped the noise and those awful words would go away.

Chapter Thirteen

K atie must have gone to sleep. When she woke up, her legs had cramp and she was very cold. It was still dark, and the moon was high in the sky. For a moment Katie felt blank. Where was she?

And then that sick feeling returned. Tom in the dungeon in total darkness — he was afraid of the dark.... Maybe it was all a bad dream. The hole in her stomach would disappear in a second, when she really woke up.

It didn't. She was awake, and this was real.

Katie shut her eyes. It was very silent, no sounds on the road. Then she heard a noise — a squeaking, shuffling noise. It was close, and getting closer. She wasn't frightened; it wasn't threatening. Snuffle ... snuffle....

Then there was another sound: twigs breaking, footsteps.... She squeezed her eyes tight. This was it. She hadn't the strength to move. At least she would be with Tom. She sat and waited.

A voice whispered in her ear, 'You're a funny badger! Have you joined the family, then?'

Katie turned around and looked up into the face of a boy a few years older than her. He was wearing a cap and his eyes were twinkling.

Katie did something she would never normally

have done: she leapt up, threw her arms around the strange boy and burst into tears. 'Help me, please help me, whoever you are....' She was gasping so much that she couldn't get any more words out.

The boy gently removed her arms from around him and made her sit down. He took a small flask out of his pocket, poured some steaming liquid into the flask-top and handed it to Katie. 'There, have some tea. You're frozen.'

As Katie gulped down the hot liquid, he studied her with his blue eyes. *Some trouble here....* He looked across at the castle. His father had told him about strange goings-on there; he wondered if this had something to do with it.

The girl was looking better. Her face had relaxed and she had stopped shivering.

'Thanks.' She handed him back the flask-top.

'I was tracking badgers — you might have heard one.' He made a snuffling noise, and Katie laughed. He thought, *She's pretty when she laughs; her little face lights up.*

'That was the strange sound I heard. I wasn't frightened, though.'

'Badgers would never hurt you — no animal would; you're sitting in their hide!'

Katie looked around and nodded. 'So that's why there's a hollow, a passageway. Thank goodness for the hide — what a good name.' She shivered again. 'If it wasn't for the badgers, I'd be locked up in that horrible castle.'

He knew he had been right: he had to help her. 'What's your name?'

'Katie.'

'I'm Patrick; people call me Patch, on account of the badgers. Okay, Katie, come home with me and —'

'But I can't leave Tom. I have to get him.'

'Tom?'

'My brother. They've got him in there — in the dungeon....' And then her arms were around Patch's neck again, and all he could hear was muffled words: '... box ... grandfather ... England....' He patted her head, and gradually the sobbing stopped.

'I'm sorry, Patch.'

He handed her a large handkerchief. She blew her nose. 'I'm sorry.'

'It's natural.' His blue eyes narrowed into wedges of ice. 'If anyone was to lay a finger on any of my brothers or sisters.... Now back to the house, and we'll work something out.'

'It has to be tonight, Patch, he'll be gone in the morning.'

Patch looked at the moon. 'Hmm.... We'd better hurry. Only a few hours left till dawn.' He put his hand under her arm. 'Come on, it's not far.'

∞

In no time at all, Katie was sitting in front of the sparkling remains of a turf fire. Patch's family were all in bed except for his father, Joe, a tall, handsome man with kind brown eyes. He made her a pot of tea and cut her a thick slice of brown bread.

She told her story — not all of it, of course; even in her desperate condition, she knew she couldn't be sure that Patch and his father were members of the Network. Joe puffed his pipe and nodded vigorously when Katie came to the goings-on in the castle.

'I'm not surprised; I thought something was up. There've been all kinds of funny yokes coming around asking questions and interfering.... You're a brave young lass and we're going to help you. D'you see that?' Joe rolled up his sleeve and held out his arm towards Katie. 'Isn't she a beauty?'

Katie saw a multicoloured snake etched into Joe's skin. When he flexed his muscles, it rippled.

She shuddered. 'Ugh — that must have been sore.'

'Aye, it was.' Joe rolled down his sleeve. 'But it was a pledge of loyalty. I was an active member of a certain Network when I was young, and I know it's been revived — and I know why; and I'm guessing that you and your brother are the two children I've heard about. Now come on; we have to rescue that young brother of yours. Patch, get the boat ready.'

Patch looked surprised. 'Boat?'

'Aye, boat. We're going to rescue that boy.' He puffed on his pipe. 'Patch doesn't know this, but I once worked in that castle. It was many years ago, when he was a baby. I'm a carpenter by trade, and when they were restoring it, I spent a while there. It was during the hard times, so the money came in handy. So, you see, I got to know every nook and cranny in that place — including the escape passage.'

Katie's eyes widened. 'Escape passage?'

Joe nodded. 'Under the dungeon.'

∞

By water the house seemed much closer to the castle than it did by land, and soon they were approaching the sinister shape. It seemed to hang over the water; it was in darkness except for one or two shafts of light from the narrow windows. Katie's fingers tightened on the side of the boat, and she thought of Tom in the darkness.

Patch took her other hand and pressed it. 'Don't worry. He'll be all right, you'll see. We boys are made of strong stuff!'

Joe had taken the oars out of the water, and he put a finger to his lips to hush them. Then he took a small paddle and glided the boat right in under the castle. Again he gave the signal for silence. All was still; the moon had sunk much lower in the sky, and to the east the sky was lightening. They hadn't much time.

Patch and Joe slowly and carefully stood up. Placing their hands on the castle wall, they moved the boat along the passage. Inch by inch, very slowly, they got to the end of the wall.

They were in a sort of pool right under the castle. Patch took out a torch and switched it on while his father paddled. They all had to keep their heads down, as the roof of the passage was very low.

Joe knew exactly where he was going. After a minute or two — though it seemed much longer to Katie — he whispered, 'Shine it up there, lad.'

The beam of the torch danced around on the rocky roof. 'It's there, it's there....' Katie could hear Joe muttering. He paddled a little bit more, and the beam stopped dancing and fell on a trapdoor. Joe put his hand on Katie's shoulder and pointed.

Katie's mouth felt dry. Suppose Tom wasn't there; suppose he had fainted with fright and was lying in a coma. Images of him flitted across her mind — rats, crows, doing unspeakable things.... She squeezed her eyes shut and then opened them. *No; he's going to be all right.*

She watched as Joe took a pair of clippers out of

his pocket and signalled to Patch to hold the boat steady. Patch gave the torch to Katie, and she shone it while Joe stood on the boat's seat and carefully cut the padlock on the trapdoor.

Katie and Patch held their breath as the seconds crept by. They could hear Joe muttering, 'Come on, ye cratur — ye sure aren't the one I put on.... Grr ... ugh ... got ye!'

Then they saw him pull the heavy lock back, and the trapdoor swung open. 'Katie, give us the torch, good girl.'

Katie gave him the torch, and he shone it into the space above the trapdoor. Yes, this was the dungeon, but it seemed to be empty — no sign of the little boy. Joe could sense Katie's anxiety and hear odd whispered words: '... is he? Where? Can you...?'

He shone the light right around once more, just to be sure. *God help her; what can we do now?*

And then he caught a faint movement, in a pile in the far corner of the dungeon. He shone the torch on the pile — wool, untreated wool. He wrinkled his nose; rats....

'Tom? Tom? Anyone there? We're friends. Katie has come back to get you.'

Then a terrified little face emerged from the wool, eyes wide and blinking. Joe could feel his heart turning into mush. *Dear Lord, the poor wee boy — terrified out of his wits.* 'Good lad — over here. Take it easy, now.'

And the little figure, more like an animal than a boy, crawled out of his nest and slowly made his way over to the trapdoor and the light.

'Come on, son.' Joe put his arms up, took the boy — light as a feather and still trembling — and handed him down to Katie.

Katie wrapped her arms around him. Was it her imagination, or had he shrunk? He seemed as thin as a wisp, and she wondered if he would ever stop shivering. 'Tom, Tommy, I'm so sorry — so, so sorry....' Tears ran down her cheeks and landed on his head. 'I should never have left you. I'll never, ever leave you again!'

Joe shut the trapdoor and moved up to the prow of the boat. He handed a second paddle to Patch. 'We haven't much time. It's getting light.' He saw that the little lad was still in a state of shock and rather dazed; he didn't know where he was. The boy's lips were bitten and chapped — one more night in there and he'd have been a goner. They had to get him away, back to the house, to some kind of safety, warmth, food and rest.

Katie kept Tom in her arms as Patch and his father moved the boat along the wall. As they came to the end of the passage, the water got lighter and the walls began to look pink; it was dawn.

When they got out from under the ledge, Patch and Joe exchanged the paddles for oars, and they were soon moving away in great sweeps. The castle looked grey in the morning light, and if anyone had been looking out of a window, they would easily have spotted the boat and its cargo. No one was looking; but they were spotted by the birds.

'Go away, will ye, ye nasty thieving yokes!' Patch waved his arm at the yellow-eyed crow that swooped down. Soon the crow was joined by another and another, until there were five or six large, black, shiny birds diving down, cawing harshly.

Katie covered Tom's head with her arms. *Why are they doing this? There's no food in the boat.... They're attacking us!*

Patch shook his fist. The crows made one more swoop and flew back to the castle.

It was when they were rounding the bend near the house that they heard the most awful cawing and croaking. It was as if all the crows in Ireland had decided to caw at once. It was an awful, hoarse, discordant sound. Then there was a single scream — a screech, really: a human screech.

Katie's grip on Tom tightened. The sentries had warned Miss Craven.

Chapter Fourteen

The next morning, while Tom slept, Katie and Patch sat in front of the fire. As Katie stared into the flickering flames, her mind was blank. The fire had put her into a trance.

Patch put his hand gently on her shoulder. 'That fire has never gone out.'

Katie blinked at him.

'Never gone out as long as we've lived in this house.'

He could see from the doubtful look on Katie's face that she was coming back to reality.

'It's true: there's always been a piece of burning turf in the grate. It means that there's always a warm fireside to come home to.'

'Patch, will Tom be all right? It was my fault. I shouldn't have left him.'

'Well, there's nothing physically wrong with him — Da had a good look at him; but he'll need lots of minding. Da thinks you should stay here for a few days, until he's back to himself.'

As Katie began to shake her head, Patch went on, 'It'll be good for both of ye. I'll show you another badger-hide and where the birds nest. I'll take Tom fishing, and ye can both help us with the hay.'

So for the next few days, Tom just slept and ate, and in time the jumpiness left him. Katie discovered new flowers and birds' nests, and one day, while Tom was fishing, Patch pointed out a beautiful greenish-blue bird perched on a branch hanging over the river; he told Katie that it was a kingfisher. Patch was very careful not to take Tom and Katie onto the roads, or even into the nearby village, in case they were noticed and tongues wagged.

Then the day came when Tom was back to his old self, and Katie asked, 'What do we do next?'

Katie, Patch and Joe were sitting around the kitchen table. Joe did what he always did when he couldn't think of an answer: he got up, went over to the fire, tapped his pipe against the stone of the hearth and then proceeded to fill it with new tobacco.

Patch scratched his head and looked at his father and then at Katie. 'I don't know. We don't even know where your grandfather lives.'

'In the West — somewhere in the West. That's not much help.' Katie smiled sheepishly.

'Well, you're really in the West now; anywhere over the Shannon is the West.' Patch's eyes widened. 'He could be down the road!'

Katie shut her eyes. There was something she'd forgotten.... 'Patch, say that word again — Sh....'

'Shannon?'

'That's it! The cabby's nephew, Rory — he lives near the Shannon.' She put her hand into the pocket where the box was and felt around. There it was — a piece of paper. She took it out, unfolded it and showed it to Patch. Patch held it up and read out: 'Rory Sweeney, Long Field, Ballymote, County Sligo.'

'His uncle said he was a traveller.'

Patch nodded. 'That'd be right. There's a big group of them; they've all got together with those

New Age hippie people....' He saw from the puzzled look on Katie's face that she had no idea what he was talking about. 'They live off herbs and potions and all that rubbish. They spend a few months here and a few months there, travelling around with their animals. They go to the horse fairs and races, specially in the summertime.'

He shook his head. 'Don't know if I'd like to be getting in with the likes of them. They're a rough lot.'

Joe was sucking contentedly on his pipe. 'That may be so, Patch my boy, but they're the ones who are likely to know who the next contact in the Network is. The Network uses people like them, because nobody pays any heed to them travelling around the country and they can move on from trouble pretty quickly. And the members of the Network are the only ones who know where your grandfather is, Katie. Now, show me that address again. I'm going into the town this afternoon; I'll make some enquiries about Rory Sweeney.'

&

It was a perfect afternoon. The sun was high and the larks twittered in the sky; bees buzzed, and there wasn't a puff of wind. Katie and Tom were helping Patch to cut the hay. While Patch cut the long green grass in deep swishes with a very dangerous-looking implement called a scythe, Katie and Tom raked the grass into neat lines so that it would dry.

It was time for a rest. Katie and Tom lay down between the lines of grass, and Katie gazed up at the sky. Her nose twitched with the dusty, burnt-toast smell of the hay. It seemed such a long time since she had lain down on that strand in Dublin and looked at the same sky while Martin the cabby was fixing his wheel; and now they were about to meet Martin's nephew. She sighed. *If only....* No, she wasn't going to say that again.

She watched Patch out of the corner of her eye. He had his shirt off, and his brown back glistened with perspiration. What strong arms he had! She smiled to herself. *Well, at least Tom and I won't be too far away, once we've found our grandfather; at least we'll all be west of the Shannon.*

She could feel her skin burning. She shut her eyes again and drifted off into a dream of sweetness and warmth, the only sounds the rhythmic swishing of the scythe and the buzzing of bees. Tom turned over and snuggled up beside her.

Suddenly another sound penetrated the lazy air: voices. Katie's heart did a flip; this was too much like last time. She tightened her arm around Tom and peered towards Patch. He was talking to a tall figure silhouetted against the sun. Thoughts raced through Katie's mind: she and Tom could cover themselves with grass....

And then the figure turned and waved, and it was Joe, back from town.

Katie leapt up and shook the dusty bits of hay from her knees. 'Come on, Tom!'

Joe had taken off his jacket and rolled up his sleeves. 'I'm going to do a bit of scything. Shame to waste a day like this.'

'Joe, Joe, did you find anything?'

Joe smiled down at Katie. 'I found him, all right. You're going to meet him tomorrow in town.' He frowned. 'You'll have to be careful; there are people asking questions. Sure, I was stopped and asked if I'd seen you two scallywags.'

Katie's eyes widened. 'Then how are we going to meet Rory? We'll be spotted.'

Joe took a puff of his pipe and spat. 'No, you won't. We'll dress you up. They'll not know you at all.'

ᘓ

That evening, Patch flung open drawer after drawer. 'It's a pity my ma's away with my sister — she'd have been good at this.' He threw a dress at Tom. 'That should fit you!'

Tom's mouth opened and his cheeks went red. He held up the dress, blue with pink spots, and looked at Patch and then at Katie. 'Me, a girl? A *girl*?'

He shook his head and stamped his foot. 'No! I won't get into this!' He threw the dress on the ground. 'No way!'

Patch stopped his rummaging and turned around to face Tom. 'Tom, you have to, it's the only way. Katie is going as your big fat sister.'

Tom was still shaking his head. Katie went over to him and put her arms around him. 'Tom, you heard what Joe said: they're here, all around the town. They're looking for us. Do you want —'

Tom looked up into Katie's eyes. 'Don't say it!' He shivered. 'All right, then, but only 'cause I don't want to be put into that dungeon again.'

Patch patted him on the shoulder. 'Good fellow. Wait till you see what we'll do with your sister!' He grinned at Katie and touched her hair. 'That'll have to go.'

Katie's face, which had already been going pink,

went bright red. She turned her head away from Patch and tried to swallow the large lump in her throat. Her hair to go.... She'd be like a plucked chicken, she'd look terrible, all bristly like the hayfield.... 'P-Patch, you don't mean it? Can't I wear a hat?'

Patch shook his head. 'No. Tom will wear one — he'll have to — but it'd draw too much attention to us if you were both wearing hats. Anyway' — he ran his fingers through her hair again — 'I don't mean we have to cut it off. I just mean we have to change the colour!'

He saw the little lines above Katie's nose deepen. 'It'll come out, the colour; it doesn't last long. My ma uses it — look!' He held up a bottle. 'Dark brown with amber tints.'

Katie smiled shyly. 'What will your mother say when she comes back and finds it all gone?'

'She's great, Ma; she won't mind at all. Now I wonder if you'd fit into a pair of trousers?' Patch held up a very big pair of blue trousers.

'Into a leg, you mean!'

'We're going to change your shape, Katie. You're going to be fat — cotton wool in your cheeks and cushions around your middle. You and Tom are going to be my cousins visiting from the city. You come down every summer.'

∞

It's a shame to wake him, Patch thought as he gazed at his father. Joe was asleep, head back, mouth open, legs stretched out. His pipe had fallen onto the floor. *He looks so peaceful, and he needs the rest.... Well, here goes.*

Patch coughed and moved a chair. His father's cheek twitched. Patch coughed again and scraped a chair across the floor.

'Wha —? What's that?' Joe's head bounced forward and he rubbed his eyes. 'Aagh, I shouldn't do that; bed is the place to sleep.' He looked over at Patch. His jaw dropped and he rubbed his eyes again. He looked at Patch. 'They're not....'

Patch grinned and nodded.

'Well, by the hokey, I'd never have guessed!'

'Uncle Joe,' said Patch, moving towards him, 'these are your nieces, come to stay from Dublin.'

Joe saw a little girl in a blue dress with pink spots. She had a pink cardigan over the dress and a straw hat pulled down over her face. She was holding the hand of a much bigger and plumper girl, a girl wearing blue trousers and a white blouse. This girl had dark-brown hair tied up in a plait; her cheeks were round, and she didn't look anything like the thin young girl with fair hair whom Joe called Katie.

He shook his head in admiration. 'Well, boyo, you've done a fine job. I wish your mother was here to see them — she'd have a great laugh. Now get out of those clothes, and off to bed with ye; ye'll have to be as bright as buttons tomorrow!'

After they'd gone, Joe sat back in his chair and thought over his afternoon in town. He had told Patch and the children that there were strange goings-on, but he hadn't told them the full story. He didn't want to scare them.

There were at least a dozen tourist guides about — far more than usual. The council offices were closed, and there were rumours of great comings and goings. The whole town had gone quiet and there was an atmosphere of fear. Joe wondered if it was safe to bring Katie and Tom into town at all. *But looking at them tonight — sure, they're different children entirely; different enough....*

He hoped they could fool those guides in their dark glasses and capeens.

Chapter Fifteen

The next morning, a fine haze covered everything. Patch groaned; another scorcher.

'You're going to bake in those clothes.
Whatever you do, don't take off your hat, Tom;
luckily it'll come in handy in the sun. Katie, you're
just going to be very, very hot with those cushions!'

Katie tried to smile, but the cotton wool in her
cheeks made her look like a hamster. Joe came out
to wave goodbye; after hugging Katie and Tom, he
clasped Patch's arm. 'Careful now, boyo. Don't
speak unless you're spoken to. They're your cousins
from the city; no need for anything else. Now good
luck to you all, and God be with you.'

Katie looked back as the pony-trap made its way
down the narrow track. She waved until the tall
figure and the whitewashed cottage faded out of
sight, and all she could see was a puff of smoke
rising straight up into the still air.

She felt for Tom's hand. Off again.... When would
they ever reach their grandfather and home?

If only Patch could come with them. He'd mind
them. Maybe he could come to the travellers; but it
would be unfair to ask.... Katie shut her eyes and
leant back against the leather seat.

They were clopping along at a good pace. Patch
turned around.

'All right back there? A mile or two and we're there.'

Katie smiled and nodded. Maybe this was the time to ask him. But she couldn't — she'd have to take the cotton wool out of her cheeks. *I'll leave it. It wouldn't be fair, anyway; he's done enough for us.*

'Patch, Patch!' Tom was leaning forward, tapping Patch on the back.

'Yes?'

'You're bringing us to meet Rory?'

'That's right.'

'Patch, I want you to stay with us. Come with us to the travellers — please, please, please!'

Katie squeezed Tom's hand. Sometimes he did know what she was thinking. She felt like putting her hands over her ears to block out Patch's reply.

'I don't know. I have to get back to my da. He needs me on the farm; that hay has to be built into cocks.... I don't know.' Patch slowed the horse down. 'Sure, Rory'll look after you, and once you get to his camp....'

He scratched his head and looked around at Katie; he saw her spaniel eyes pleading.

'Ah, sure, there'll be no harm done if I'm not back till tomorrow!'

Katie relaxed. As the clopping got faster again, she saw hedges of honeysuckle and fuchsia, with their dainty ballerina flowers, pass by in a haze of purples and yellows. A lark shot up into the air and a black-and-white sheepdog blinked at them from his farmhouse gate. Katie felt so content that she even stopped noticing the wads of cotton wool. She had Patch for another day.

'Nearly there.' Pulling at the reins, Patch turned around and smiled at them. 'Not long now.'

Katie stretched her arms and felt her plait: good, it was still in place. As she moved her head back, she noticed two black specks in the sky. Something about them made her uneasy.

She tugged at Patch's shirt. 'Patch, look, just ahead — up in the sky. What are they?'

The specks were getting bigger, and it was Tom who uttered the word first.

'Crows! They're crows. Ugh, I hate them!'

Patch gave him a friendly punch. 'Tom, Ireland is full of them. Sure, they've as much right to fly as that lark up there.'

Katie still felt uneasy. The crows seemed to be flying straight at them, and now they were so near that she could see their long beaks and their nasty yellow eyes.

Tom shivered. 'I don't like them, Patch, no matter what you say, and I'll never forget those horrible crows at the castle.'

'Anyway, they're gone now, so they are. Look, we're practically there.' Patch was pointing ahead, at roofs glinting among the trees.

'They're not, they're — look, Patch!' Tom pressed himself up against Patch's back. Directly above them, the two crows were circling and swooping. Katie put her hands over her head.

'Caw ... caw ... caw....'

Katie screamed as one of the crows swooped down and took off Tom's hat in its beak.

'Whoa, whoa there.' Patch stopped the pony and trap and stood up on the seat. 'Get away, go on with ye — get away, ye thieving yokes!'

'Caw ... caw....' With a beat of their blue-black wings, the crows flew off into the trees, dropping Tom's hat onto the road as they went.

Patch leapt down from the trap and ran across to where the straw hat sat in the middle of the road. He waved it at Tom as he ran back. 'Well, Tom, just as well that crow had a slippery beak, or we'd have had to go back to the house and get another!' He shook his head. 'I've never seen a bird as cheeky as that. Now magpies and jackdaws will thieve anything that shines — but a crow....'

Katie shook his arm. 'Patch, don't you see, they're the castle crows, the crows from the castle — remember when we were in the boat? I know they are. They've been looking for us. They're on patrol — remember the story I told you, about the sentries?'

'They're after us, Katie — they'll tell her, and she'll lock us up again....' Tom threw himself on the floor of the trap. 'I hate this! I don't want to see our grandfather. I want to go back to Joe. Patch, take us back, please!'

Katie bent down and put her hand on his back. 'Tom, get up. We'll be all right. Patch said he'd stay with us. Think about it: birds can't talk.'

'Katie's right, Tom. Now get up, be a brave fella. I said I'd stay with you and wait till you meet Rory; they say his father's a real strong man.'

Patch helped Katie to pull Tom onto the seat, and then they were off again towards the town. For the remainder of their journey, nothing more appeared in the sky; even the larks were gone, and all was silent.

'Whoa there....' Patch slowed the pony down to a trot as they entered the town. 'Now careful, you two. Tom, remember you're a girl!'

Tom stuck his tongue out at Patch.

'Tom, you can't do that — you'll make everyone look at you!'

'I know, that's why I'm doing it now!'

Patch grinned. Tom was back to his old self.

They trotted down the main street. Katie saw brightly coloured shop-fronts, blue, red, yellow and green; all the shops had boxes outside, displaying their goods — vegetables and fruits, books, flowers.... There was even a shop selling nothing but candles.

'Ice-cream!' Tom pointed to a café that had a red-and-blue awning outside. Right across the awning, the words 'ICE-CREAM' sprang out in creamy-white letters.

'Ooh....' Katie felt the perspiration on her cheeks. 'I'd love an ice-cream!'

Patch nodded. 'As soon as we get Dolly here parked. We're meeting Rory in that café, so you can have an ice-cream then.'

Five minutes later, with Dolly safely tied up and munching a bag of oats, Patch led Katie and Tom towards the café.

There were very few locals about, but they still had to push their way along the narrow pavements, which were full of tourists taking photographs of everything in sight: 'Look at those oranges! ... And what about the tomatoes? ... I must take one of those books, they'll never believe it!'

Katie and Tom stopped to gaze into a window that was brimming over with cakes and buns. Tom licked his lips and pointed to a glossy chocolate-covered cake. Katie had her eyes on some pretty cakes covered with white icing. She was just about to say something to Tom when she heard Patch's voice — and he wasn't talking to them.

'Yes, Officer Quigley, Da's fine. Yes, busy savin' the hay....'

Katie turned around and saw a big, fat man in

uniform. He had a red face, which he was rubbing from time to time with a greyish handkerchief. He was looking at her and Tom in a puzzled way.

'Eh, these are my cousins, down from Dublin — on Ma's side.'

The guard took his cap off and began wiping his head. 'Well, ye must be feeling the heat in all them clothes! Ye should go for a swim; it'd cool ye down.' He slapped Patch on the back. 'Get on with ye, now; I've got work to do. We've been told to watch out for illegals.'

'Oh?'

Katie could feel Tom's nails biting into her hand. She wanted to hear what the guard had to say, but at the same time she wanted to run. She turned to the shop window again, pulling Tom around so that they had their backs to the guard.

'Girl and boy. Don't know how they slipped through Dublin. Anyway, the powers that be want them fast, so I'd better be off. Will you take those two in there and get them a bun — their tongues must be hanging out! Here....' He threw some coins into Patch's hand. 'Get them on me. Be seein' ye!'

Patch waved and took Katie by the arm. 'Come on, you two, let's find Rory and get you out of this town as soon as possible.'

'Patch, can't I have a cake, please?' Tom pulled at Patch's sleeve. Katie didn't say anything, but the warm, yeasty smell coming out of the bakery was making her hungry.

'Look, Tom, I'll get you an ice-cream like I said I would, but we have to get away from here. The tourist guide over there is givin' us funny looks, and now we know that they're on to us....' He shook his head. 'I can't believe it was the crows.'

Katie looked across the street, and, sure enough, there was one of those horrible green-suited guides. He was talking to a couple with a camera, and they were all staring at the three children. Katie forgot her hunger. She shivered, even though it was hot. 'Yes — quick, Tom, let's go.'

From across the street, a voice shouted at them, 'Hey, there!'

Patch hissed, 'What are we going to do? It looks like they're coming over!'

Katie looked at Tom's skirt and felt her own cushioned stomach. 'We can't run, they'd catch us....'

The guide and the couple were crossing the street. Patch, Katie and Tom all froze. It was as if they were stuck to the pavement.

The guide approached them, smiling. 'Look, sorry, but we have a request.'

Katie tried to smile.

The tourist waved his camera. 'Gee, you two girls are so cute and Irish-looking, I just gotta take a shot for the folks back home. Just stand right there, won't take a minute.' He stood back and held up the camera; *click....* The guide waved, and they disappeared into the crowd.

Katie could feel rivers of perspiration running down her face. She felt like falling down in a heap on the pavement and melting.

Patch was in command again. 'Come on, we have to hurry up. Rory'll be waiting.' He gently pulled Katie's arm. 'You look as if you need an ice-cream.'

Tom was licking his lips. 'Can't wait. Let's go!'

After the glaring sun and the dusty street, the café was dark and cool. There was a faint murmur from customers sitting around the tables, but other-wise it was quiet. Patch moved ahead and spoke to a figure leaning against the counter.

When he called Katie over, she saw a stocky boy of about Patch's height; he had curly hair, a fat little nose and a face covered with freckles. He put out his hand and gave Katie a wide smile.

'Hi, Katie, I'm Rory. Hi, Tom!' He gave Tom a friendly thump on his arm. 'How're ye doin'?'

'I'd love an ice-cream. Patch promised us —'

'Right, ice-creams all round.' Rory put money on the counter, and, as if by magic, four large white ice-cream cones appeared, creamy and glistening with flecks of ice. Katie felt her mouth watering. But how was she going to eat it with those stupid wads of cotton wool in her mouth? She'd have to take them out.

She looked at Patch and pointed at her cheeks and then at the ice-cream. Patch looked puzzled for a moment; then he nodded. 'Rory, we'll go over to that table in the back corner while Katie eats her ice-cream.'

'All right, but we can't be long; we're already late. We're all moving off tonight.'

'Already?'

'Yes, there's the horse-races tomorrow at Sligo, on the strand. We never miss them.'

Patch put his head back for a moment and gazed at the ceiling. 'It's a relief, that is, 'cause I think they're on to us. So the sooner we move from here, the better. But ...' He looked at Katie. 'I promised Katie I'd stay; but if you're moving, I'm not so sure....'

Katie had sat down and started carefully taking the cotton wool out of her cheeks, but when she heard Patch, she stopped and clamped her mouth shut. A tear rolled down her cheek, but before she could say anything, Patch put out his hand and wiped it away. 'I'll come, I'll come to Sligo. I've always wanted to go to those strand races.'

Katie sniffed and finished taking the cotton wool out of her cheeks. Tom gave her a grateful kick under the table.

∞

When they reached the place where the travelling families were camped, Rory brought Katie and Tom into his caravan to meet his father. 'He's the head of all the families camped here,' he told them.

Rory's father, Dan, was huge, with a shiny bald head and a bushy red beard. The beard flowed over a long purple garment which was tied at the waist by a woven belt. Katie's and Tom's eyes fastened on the drawing on the front of the garment. It was nearly covered by the beard; but they could see enough of it to tell that it was a B, adorned and entwined with flowers and calves.

'Ye like my shirt?' grinned Dan. 'I put it on specially for you. You're in safe hands now. Come here....' He pulled Katie and Tom over to the window. 'Look over there. D'ye see where the sun is setting?'

Katie and Tom looked out at the silhouette of a mountain against the pink sky.

'That's the West. Beyond that mountain is an even bigger mountain, Knocknarea, and that's where Queen Maeve is buried. That's where your grandfather lives, in the shadow of that mountain. It's a very ancient place. It's too dangerous for him to come here, so we'll take you to him. He's expecting you; we'll send him a message tonight to tell him that you're safe. D'ye have something with you?'

Katie nodded.

'That's all right. I don't want to know. You're in safe hands now, and the sooner we leave this place, the better....' Suddenly he let go of Katie and Tom and returned to the window. 'Aah — maybe I spoke too soon!'

Katie could hear it now: a noise of barking and shouting and horses whinnying. Dan quickly lifted up the tops of the two beds that stood on either side of the caravan. 'Quick, in you get, girl — in there beside those blankets. Tom, you go in that one.'

Katie buried her head in a pillow as she felt the wooden top clunk down on top of her. She could hear muffled sounds — a knocking on the door — then Dan's voice: 'All right, I'm coming! Hold on!'

Then another voice, a woman's: 'Health inspector ... complaints ... refuse ... rats ... take a look....'

Katie shivered. She would have recognised that voice anywhere. Miss Craven!

The voice was getting louder, clearer, coming nearer. 'Hmm ... must say, clean and tidy. Are these beds comfortable?' And then Katie felt the bed creak on top of her, and she could smell perfume, sweet and cloying — she was going to sneeze!

'... quite comfortable....'

'Aah ... aah ...' Katie couldn't hold it in any longer. 'Achoo!'

'... noise?'

Dan gave an enormous sneeze. 'I must be getting something.'

Katie lay still as a stone. She couldn't move.

At last she heard Miss Craven get up from the bed and click her way down the caravan. 'Careful of rats, Mr Sweeney; they're everywhere.... I may return in the morning with my team.'

The door slammed. Silence.

Katie shut her eyes and counted. She suddenly thought of Tom in a dark, confined space. Her heart thumped. Out — she had to get out — she had to see him! *Ten, eleven, twelve....* Deep breaths; Miss Craven could still be there waiting. Dan would lift the top of the bed if it was safe. *Fifteen, sixteen....* And then light — the top lifted.

'All right, you can come out; she's gone. Health inspector, my foot! She's some lady — the coldest eyes I ever did see. And she was looking for something, someone.'

'Miss Craven, it was Miss Craven — the crows warned her.... Tom —' Katie tumbled out onto the floor and flipped up the other bed's top.

Tom's white face stared up at her with glassy, unseeing eyes. Katie screamed.

Dan moved Katie aside. 'Don't worry, he'll be all right. Let's get him out. He's in shock — have you ever seen a frightened rabbit? Now get me a rug, he needs to be warmed up; and then make him a big mug of hot tea.'

When Katie came back with the tea, Tom's colour was returning and his pupils had shrunk to their normal size. He was still trembling, though.

'Tom —' Katie kissed his head. 'It's all right. Miss Craven came again, but she didn't find us. We're nearly there, Tom, we're nearly at Grandfather's!'

After a while, Dan handed Tom over to Katie. 'He'll be fine. I have to go now, to organise the move. I'll send Rory and Patch in to you. When you wake up in the morning, we'll be on the other side of that mountain, by the sea — and we'll be away from that woman and her like!'

Chapter Sixteen

The next day, when the four of them arrived at Cumeen Strand in Sligo, the tide was in. Tom groaned. He had been looking forward to the races.

'Are they going to race, Patch? I want to see them running on the sand. It won't be the same if they're in a field.'

'Don't worry, they'll be racing this afternoon; the tide'll go out just as fast as it came in. Anyhow, you can have some fun at the fair. Come on, we'll go and see how many stalls are up.'

Even though it was early, there was a lot of noise and commotion. Families were arriving in their pony-traps, and Tom noticed a good many boys of his age running and jumping around the stalls. He was delighted that, as there were no tourist guides or guards in little Cumeen Strand, he didn't have to wear that stupid dress and hat and act like a girl — especially with all these boys about!

'Look, Tom!' Patch was pointing into the distance. 'See, they're putting up the swingboats. They're great fun: you get into them, two to a boat, and pull the ropes, and then you're up in the air — it's just like a swing. You have to be with someone about your own size, so you and Katie could go in one —'

Tom couldn't wait. 'I'll go and get her!'

'They're not ready yet; it'll be another hour. Anyway, Katie's not in the caravan, she's over in that field looking at the horses with Rory.'

∞

'Oh, they're beautiful, Rory.' Katie's eyes were shining as she stroked a particularly handsome black horse. His nose felt velvety and soft.

Rory gave her some sugar-lumps. 'Here, put out your hand flat and he'll take one. Don't worry, he won't bite.'

Katie put out her hand and felt the horse's teeth gently flicker along her palm as he took the sugar. It was like being given a sloppy, wet kiss.

'I'd love to ride him,' she said wistfully, gazing up into the horse's liquid brown eyes.

Rory shook his head. 'You couldn't ride one of these. They're racehorses; they'd go far too fast and you'd fall off. Maybe your grandfather'll have horses.'

Katie bit her lip and turned away. Rory had reminded her of the real world — the world of uncertainty and danger which, just for a moment, she had forgotten.

'Katie, Katie!' Tom was tearing towards her. Her breath stuck in her throat: *Not more bad news.*

'Katie, Katie, they've swings here, swingboats! You have to come with me; Patch is too big.'

Patch, who had caught up with Tom, winked at Katie. 'Rory and I will go in the other one, and we'll have a race. We'll have to wait a while, though; they're not ready yet.'

∞

So, with the sun getting high in the sky and the smell of salt and horse in the air, and feeling safe with Patch and Rory, Katie and Tom strolled around the field, looking at the horses. There were about twelve of them. Katie had already decided on her favourite: the gentle-looking grey one with the fluffy white mane.

Patch pointed to another horse, which was as black as night. He was bigger than the others, and even while he munched the grass, he pawed at the ground with his hoof and occasionally threw his head back and whinnied.

'I wouldn't go on him even if I was paid!' muttered Patch. 'He'll probably win, but he's temperamental. You'd need a strong rider to control him.'

Tom was becoming fidgety. He wanted to go on the swingboats. 'Patch, they're up — they've got them up. Can we have a ride?'

Katie had gone over to the edge of the field to look at the strand. She saw that the tide had ebbed, almost as if it had been sucked away.

She felt Patch come up behind her. 'Patch, it's gone out so quickly!'

'Yes, and it'll come in again in no time at all; there's no stopping the tide. So we only have about half an hour until the races begin.'

'Don't the horses get stuck in the sand?'

Patch laughed. 'Not at all, they're used to it; they're specially trained. Besides, the sun will soon be at its hottest, so it'll dry out. Horses love water, Katie; the horses round here go for swims every day.'

Katie was happy. She felt Patch's shoulder touch hers. She could smell the salty air, hear the gulls cry. She and Tom were near the end of their journey. She put her hand into her pocket; the box was still there. Tomorrow, or the next day, they would be with their grandfather on the other side of the mountain, and she would hand over the box. Nothing could stop them now.

'Patch, Katie!' Tom's voice echoed in the clear air. 'Hurry up! I want to go in the boats. Come on; Rory said the races could be starting soon, so we don't have much time.'

Rory had already lifted Tom into a swingboat, and he was pulling at the rope in excitement. 'Quick, quick, Katie! We're going to have a race to see who goes higher. You have to pull my rope, and I pull yours.'

Soon the boat was swinging rhythmically, slowly moving further out from the posts and rising gently into the air. Katie looked over at Patch and Rory. Their boat was going much faster and they were shouting and roaring.

'Katie, pull harder! I want to get as high as them!' Tom's face was red and perspiration was running down his arms.

Katie wasn't going to pull any harder. She was enjoying the rhythmic movement, being up here in the sky — she could even see a lark. Pull, pull, up and up.... She shut her eyes for a moment. The clamour and noise of the fair seemed far away. She felt she was really in a boat on the sea — up and down on the waves....

She opened her eyes, looked down, and froze. Her hands slipped on the rope; the boat began to wobble.

'What are you doing? Hold on to the rope!' Patch and Rory were shouting at her. 'Get hold of it quick! The boat's going too fast; Tom can't hold on —'

Katie opened her mouth, and four words came

out in a scream against the wind: 'The man in white!'

Patch had got out of his boat and was on the ground, pulling Katie's boat down. He put his arm around her. 'It's all right, you just imagined it — it's easy to mix up shapes and colours from the air. You were going too fast, you were dreamin' — it's easy to get carried away in those boats....'

Katie shook her head and sobbed, 'No, it's him. I couldn't make a mistake about him. And besides, there's a woman with him — I think it's Miss Craven, but I only saw him properly, in the white, the.... Oh, I thought we were safe at last — they wouldn't find us here! Oh, Patch, what will we do?'

'They haven't seen you yet, so you're still safe. They must have got a tip-off, but they don't know for definite. Where were they?'

'Near ... near the s-stalls.'

'Right, we'll not go near the stalls, we'll go over to where the horses are. There'll be a lot of people around there, because the first race is due to start. Come on.'

The four of them left the swingboats and crept over towards the starting post of the first race. Katie heard the excited voices of the crowd and the impatient whinnying of the horses, but she couldn't enjoy it any more; she was too frightened.

She looked at Tom. His face had gone all white and pinched again. She clutched his hand. 'We'll be all right, Tom, we've got Patch and Rory.'

'Five minutes to the first race.' The cheery microphone voice made them jump. 'Five minutes, please. Place your bets. Last bets, please.'

They were at the starting post, beside the horses. Katie hung on to Patch's sleeve with one hand and clutched Tom with the other. Her favourite horse, the grey, stamped impatiently; her rider hadn't come yet.

The next few seconds passed in a blink. Tom was pulling her sleeve. 'Katie, they're here — the man in white, Miss Craven — they've seen us! Patch, they're heading this way —'

Patch looked over to where Tom was pointing. There they were, the pair of them. There was only one thing to do.

'Rory, get up on that horse with Tom — me and Katie'll go on the grey — and get away from here as fast as you can.'

Patch took the reins of the grey. 'Shh, girl, shh....' He gently rubbed her neck. Then he lifted Katie up onto the saddle and leapt up himself.

'I'm behind you,' he said. 'Hold on to that mane.' People were shouting at them, and two men in jockey caps were waving their whips in the air, but it didn't matter: they were off. 'Go on, gee-up!'

Katie saw Rory and Tom out of the corner of her eye, just behind her; and then they were racing along the strand, with the wind whistling through her hair. Other horses were passing them, and she realised that they were in the first race. She could see the other horses racing around the poles that were stuck in a circle in the sand. If she hadn't felt so scared, it would have been a beautiful sight — the horses racing through the shadows on the sand. She was scared of falling off and she was scared of the man in white, but they were racing away from him; he and Miss Craven were left behind.

'Don't worry, you won't fall off.' She could feel Patch's breath on her neck. 'Just hold on to the mane.'

Then Patch looked behind him, and there was the man in white, on the big black horse. 'Easy now,

Katie — don't look, keep holding on — but we're being followed. He's on the big black horse.'

Katie screamed. She felt her fingers loosening on the mane.

'Katie, didn't I tell you about that horse? It won't be long until he throws that man off. The thing is, I want him to throw him off in the right place. Now hold on tight, I'm going to change direction.'

Patch pulled the reins to the left. They were still galloping along at a great pace, but Katie turned around for a moment and caught a glimpse of white on black just behind them.

'Easy, girl, easy....'

Katie saw that Patch was heading out beyond the poles, away from the other horses. She hoped that the man in white would follow them, that he wouldn't keep on after Tom and Rory, because she knew that Patch must have a plan.

Don't follow them, she prayed. She turned around again and saw that, indeed, the blur of white on black was following her and Patch out beyond the poles.

Patch could feel the horse tiring; she was beginning to snort. 'Go, girl, go on!' They were well beyond the poles, still heading around in a circle, and Katie could see that they were dangerously near the sea. They were riding along a narrow spit of sand with a channel of deep water on the left.

Slowing down the horse, Patch whispered, 'Don't worry, I want him to follow us along here. I want him to think he's got us. He'll be going at such a gallop that he'll be thrown off.'

Sure enough, as the man in white came racing towards them on the narrow spit, his horse reared, and the man in white fell off into the channel of water. The last Katie saw of him was the top of a bony head and two white arms waving about.

'He'll not drown, but he'll be very wet and sorry for himself. We're safe; we'll be away from here by the time he's dried off.'

Katie leant back against Patch in relief. 'You've saved us again, Patch.'

When they got back to the finishing post, they could see Rory and Tom waving and clapping. They were pointing to a figure in a boat, a figure with glasses and long fair hair flapping in the wind: Miss Craven, red-faced and disgruntled and rowing very badly.

'That'll keep her busy,' muttered Patch. 'Jump down, Katie.' He took Katie's hand and helped her to the ground.

Katie stroked the grey's nose. 'Thank you, thank you for saving us.'

Rory put his hand on Patch's arm. 'Come on, Patch, Da wants to see us. There's news from across the mountain.'

Chapter Seventeen

ews from across the mountain! Katie was half-running to catch up with Patch.

'Patch, what does Rory mean? It can't be more bad news!' Her safe feeling, the feeling she had had ever since the man in white sank beneath the waves, disappeared. Of course there were others, and they wanted the box badly.

Katie was panting. It wasn't just the running; it was the fear. She caught hold of Patch's shirt. 'Patch, you'll stay with us, won't you? You'll not go back, not yet — you'll stay until we reach Grandfather?'

Patch didn't say anything and he didn't stop in his stride. They were nearing the caravan.

'Patch —!' Katie gave a plaintive cry.

Patch stopped and held out his hand. 'Katie, I'm sorry; I have to get back. I'll come and visit you. It isn't far — a day's ride.'

Katie took a deep breath. 'I'm sorry for behaving like this. It's selfish of me. I don't know what we'd have done without you.'

Patch rubbed her shoulder. 'Listen, it's all right. You've been through a lot; but it's all over now — well, nearly. Look, we've got a visitor. That's what Rory meant when he said there was news from across the mountain.' He pointed towards the caravan.

Rory and Tom were already at the caravan door,

patting a big white horse. Rory nodded towards the door, and Patch pushed Katie forward. 'Go on in. I'll wait here with Rory and Tom.'

He saw Katie's face fall. 'Oh, all right, I'll come in with you. But there's nothing to worry about; it'll just be news from your grandfather. He knows ye're here; Rory's da sent word to him yesterday.' He gave her a gentle little push up the caravan steps. 'Go on, now.'

Katie knocked at the door.

'Come in, come in.' Dan had a booming voice. Katie saw that he was sitting at the table, across from a tall woman with thick copper-coloured hair. She wore a purply-brown shirt-dress, and a silver pendant hanging around her neck glittered and shone. She turned her head and smiled at Katie.

When Katie saw the wide curly mouth and the long amber eyes, she felt that she knew the woman; she'd met her before. There was something about the way she put her hand up to her hair.... But where ...? The circus? The boat?

'Katie, this is Tara.'

Tara got up and drew Katie towards her. 'You think you've seen me before, don't you?'

Katie nodded.

'Come here.' Tara brought Katie over to a mirror which hung over a chest of drawers. 'Now look in there!'

Katie looked. She saw two matching noses, long and straight; and when she smiled, the other smile was exactly the same.

'Katie, dear, I'm your aunt.'

Katie gasped. 'And you — you remind me of Dad.'

She felt a tear roll down her cheek, and then Tara's arms were around her.

'I know, I know. I miss him too. When we were little, we did so much together.'

'Just like me and Tom,' Katie sniffed.

'Just like you and Tom. And then he went away, and we didn't hear from him again until he sent us the message about you.'

'And I never knew that I had an auntie.'

'He was afraid, you see, Katie; he didn't want to put us in any more danger.' Tara kissed the top of Katie's head. 'Oh, Katie, Katie, you and Tom are nearly home now. Your grandfather is so looking forward to seeing you ... and you've got something very important to give him.'

Katie stiffened and pulled away from Tara. She looked into her face again — so like her father's, so like her own; but she felt uneasy. What if this was a trick? After all they'd been through — to fail now....

'I — I do have something ... but....'

Tara patted Katie's shoulder. 'I know: the Alphabet Network. You're quite right. Here.' She put her hand up to her throat and took the pendant in it. 'Look at that. What do you see?'

Katie stared at the silver pendant and made out an ornamental design of a deer entwined with a D.

'My code-name is Deer.'

Katie blushed. 'I'm sorry, Tara, but we were told ...'

'You're quite right.' Tara tossed her hair back. 'Now, we're going to have to be on our way. Your grandfather is dying to see you; and besides, time is against us. Can you ride a horse?'

Katie looked round at Patch, who was sitting quietly in the corner. He shook his head.

Tara frowned. 'I can take one behind me on my horse, but not two.'

Patch started to get up. 'I'll go with you.'

Katie threw herself on him. 'Oh, thank you, Patch — but what about Joe?'

Patch looked over at Dan.

'I know, your da's in the middle of saving the hay. I'll tell you what: I'll send Rory and one of his pals over. They can go this evening.' Dan smiled at Patch. 'I can see you have important affairs of state to see to!'

Tara rubbed her hands. 'All right, Patch, you take Katie on your horse and I'll take Tom on mine. It's only an hour's ride from here.'

Suddenly Katie's arms felt tingly. She had come so far, and here she was, standing beside her aunt. Her aunt! An aunt she hadn't even known she had! The grey landscape of England and that awful train journey seemed such a long time ago, and so much had happened since.

She shuddered. They'd be safe now. Safe forever. They were practically there; and they weren't on their own any more. Patch and Tara were with them.

Chapter Eighteen

Most of the ride was uphill. It seemed longer than an hour. They were skirting the edge of the mountain, the same mountain that Dan had pointed out the day before. Tara told them that it was Maeve's mountain; Maeve had been a warrior queen, and she was buried under the mound of stones on top of the mountain.

They stopped beside a mountain stream for a drink. Tara knelt down by the stream and cupped the water in her hands. 'Go on, it's delicious!' And it was, icy cold and faintly brackish.

Katie watched Tom. His eyes were shining, and every now and then he glanced at Tara in an adoring way.

'Katie, Tara's been telling me all sorts of things. I'm really going to love living with Grandfather. There's a school nearby, and lots of horses; we can learn to ride.'

He shyly took Tara's hand. 'I can't believe you're our aunt. I always thought aunts were fat little ladies with horrible glasses and warts!'

Tara threw her head back and laughed. 'Enough of that, Tom. Look, d'you see over there?' She had stood up and was pointing towards the sunset. 'Another ten minutes and we're home. I didn't tell you, did I, that your grandfather lives on a little

island in the middle of a lake? It's not really a lake
— but I'll tell you more about that later. We'd better
get going now.'

And so they set off once more, heading down now
along the mountain tracks. Katie didn't feel scared.
The horses knew exactly where they were going.

'Whoa there.' Tara brought her horse to a stop
and Katie saw Tom jump down.

'Katie, a fort — there's a fort up ahead! Look, it's
in the lake!'

Tara laughed as Katie and Patch walked their
horse up beside her.

'It's not really a fort, although it does look like
one. Your grandfather loves the old ways, and that's
why he built the house on this little island. About
twelve hundred years ago, or even more, the people
who lived here made the island: they laid down
stones in the shallow water until they rose above
the surface, and then covered them with wood.
That's why it's called a *crannóg*: *crann* is the Irish
word for wood. Then they built a wall of wood to
protect themselves from attack.'

'Wasn't there a special way across?' asked Patch.
'Some kind of secret path, with stepping-stones?'

'You're right, but we usually use boats, though I
do remember my father bringing me over that way
when I was a child. Anyway, we're nearly there; down
the rest of this hill, and we'll be home before dark.'

It didn't take them long to get down to the edge of
the lake. The sun had practically disappeared, and
there was a dusty pink tinge to the air. Katie could
hear the silence, broken only by the *pweet-pweet* of
a night bird.

Patch lifted Katie down from the horse, and they
followed Tara and Tom into a nearby field. There were

at least six other horses in the field. Tara and Patch removed the saddles and bridles; Tara gave their horses a slap on their rumps, and they cantered off to join the others. She left the saddles in a barn at the entrance to the field.

Tara kissed Katie.

'Well, this is it: the end of your journey.'

Katie felt an immense relief. She wouldn't have to worry about that wretched box any more. She wouldn't have to worry about Tom. They were both going to be looked after.

She put her hand into her back pocket and took out the box. It looked so normal — just a smooth wooden sliver of a thing.

She showed it to Tara. 'Here it is. This is the box; this is what they want.'

Tara took it and held it in the palm of her hand. 'Your father's message mentioned this box, but he didn't say what was in it. Here, put it back in your pocket. You've kept it safe until now; you can give it to your grandfather.'

She took a torch down from a shelf. 'It's getting dark — just dark enough for him to see the torch signal and send a boat across. Come on, let's go to the edge of the lake.'

When they got there, Patch shook his head and looked at Tara. 'I don't know too much about boats, but I wouldn't say you'd get a boat across on that.'

Even though the visibility was poor, Katie could also see that the water was quite shallow.

'Patch is right: the water just covers the bottom. How could a boat possibly come over?'

Tara sat down on the grass and smiled up at them. 'Do you know what a punt is?'

They shook their heads.

'It's a flat boat that can travel on very shallow water. You move it with a pole.'

'Why can't we just walk across?' said Tom, taking his shoes off. 'Just paddle.'

Tara caught his arm. 'Careful, Tom. If you were to walk in there, you'd sink into the mud and it would suck you down. The only way you could walk across is by the secret path, and I can't remember it — it's been so long. Father knows, of course, but he's the only one.'

Patch was shaking his head. 'They really were smart, the fellas who built this *crannóg* — built it in a lake that isn't really a lake, and only one secret path to it.'

Tara smiled at him. 'Well, that's the way it is now, but back in the eighth century it actually was a lake. Anyway, I'll give the signal to let them know it's us, and they'll come.' She held up the torch and flashed it three times. Katie watched the walled islet in front of them and soon saw an answering three flashes.

'Good, they know we're here.' Tara put the torch into her pocket. 'I'm sure you're all starving. There'll be a celebration tea to welcome you; and Patch, you can get a good night's sleep before you take off in the morning.'

Katie had forgotten that Patch would be leaving, and her face fell.

Patch gave her a friendly punch. 'Katie, I'm only an hour's ride away, and when things settle down, you and Tom can come and stay.'

'Look, look!' Tom was dancing up and down. 'They're coming, they're coming!'

Sure enough, a tall figure with a long pole in his hands was pushing a flat boat towards them.

'Shh....' Patch stiffened. 'What's that noise?'

Against the background of silence and lapping water, Katie could hear the discordant sound of a motor — a car!

Tara clutched Tom's hand. 'Nobody from around here has a car....'

The noise was getting louder, and bright white lights beamed straight at them. The punt wobbled, and the boatsman was left clinging to the side. Tara grabbed the pole.

Katie looked around and was blinded by the dazzling light of a jeep's two huge, fish-eyed lamps.

Doors opened, voices sounded in the night stillness. She felt sick. *I knew it, I knew they'd come, even when we're this close.*

She felt in her pocket. The box was warm and smooth. Her hand tightened around it. *They're not having it.*

She heard Tara's voice calling, 'Katie, come on, quickly! Your grandfather is on the secret path — move towards him!'

In front of them, as though he was walking on water, came a figure — a big, broad-shouldered figure. He was beckoning them.

And then there were other voices, and she would have recognised Miss Craven's high-pitched shriek anywhere: '— thought you'd tricked us — won't get away this time!'

Tara was shouting, 'Katie, come on!'

'In a minute,' Katie said. 'There's something I have to do.'

She took the pole from Tara and turned to face Miss Craven and the man in white. She felt calm, and everything looked very clear. A deep voice — *That must be Grandfather* — echoed behind her:

'Hold my hand, Tom, and follow me. It's just like playing hopscotch.'

Miss Craven and the man in white had managed to clamber onto some large flat stones at the edge of the lake. The man in white was in front; Miss Craven followed, holding on to his jacket. Katie reckoned that they were about five feet away.

She braced her feet firmly on a stone, gripped the pole with both hands and started counting to five. They were moving nearer; Miss Craven panted, 'We've got you now, you little brat....' The man in white reached out towards Katie.

Four ... five.... Katie gritted her teeth and stabbed the pole, with all her might, straight at the man in white. It hit him in the middle of his chest and he toppled into the lake, arms flapping, with Miss Craven still clinging to his jacket.

And then Katie was shaking all over, and Tara was holding her and whispering, 'Dear Katie, brave Katie, it's all over now....'

It was really only a short distance to the islet, which was lit up now, but Katie couldn't resist a glance back. She could just see two sinking figures, faint against the moonlight, clawing and struggling with each other as the mud sucked them down.

༄

When they walked into the welcoming light of Grandfather's doorway, they were greeted by about six dogs of various shapes and sizes. The dogs threw themselves at Grandfather and then proceeded to lick Katie, Tom and Patch all over. A huge fire burned in the fireplace.

Grandfather was a big, comfortable man with the greenest eyes Katie had ever seen. His face had all sorts of funny lines and crevices, and his longish hair curled behind his ears — *like a lion's*, thought Tom. He had spotted a lion's head on his grandfather's ring.

The room they were standing in had a high ceiling, and pictures lined the walls. Most of them were pictures of animals and trees, but there was one of a much-younger Grandfather holding the hand of a small boy.

Katie pointed at it. 'That's Tom! But how —?'

Her grandfather pulled her close. 'That's your father, when he was exactly the age Tom is now.' He kissed the top of her head. 'Katie, my dear, he gave you something for me.'

Katie put her hand into her pocket, took out the box, and placed it in her grandfather's palm.

'You're a brave girl. Now let's see what's inside.'

Katie watched as he slid his thumbnail around the edge of the box. She heard a click, and the box sprang open.

She watched her grandfather's face; he smiled and nodded. 'That's it — the last piece of the jigsaw puzzle, the evidence we need.' He handed the box to Tara. 'What do you think?'

Tara put her hand over her mouth and gasped. 'Séamus Slevin and Togo Yukinora!'

Katie looked puzzled. All this fuss over a silly old photo? Tara passed the box to Katie; in it, sure enough, was a photograph of two men smiling at each other and shaking hands.

'But, Grandfather, that's the little fat man who was in the castle! He was with Miss Craven. He was horrible!'

Grandfather nodded. 'That would fit.... I'll explain in a minute, child. But first of all, Tara, take the photograph and fax a copy to our First Minister. I'm sure he'll be very interested in seeing his Minister for Tourism and Finance shaking hands with the greatest crook in the world.

'Katie, Togo Yukinora is the head of the world's greediest corporation. He is responsible for the desert lands in Europe and Britain. His companies have used up all of their resources. Now he has his eye on Ireland, because we are the only country in Europe with any natural resources left. We have Nature to thank for that — so long as we don't interfere with her.'

'I remember the Abbot of that monastery telling me about him,' Katie said.

Her grandfather nodded. 'I knew about Slevin and his dirty dealings years ago, but I had no proof. But now, thanks to your father....' He held Katie closer. 'Katie, your father was killed by Tartarus. It was no accident; one of our friends saw him being pushed off that bridge. They knew he had the photograph, but he wouldn't tell them where it was.... Tomorrow morning, this picture will be on the front of every newspaper in the country. This hoodlum Yukinora has managed to bribe Séamus Slevin with millions of pounds.'

'To do what?' asked Patch.

'To sell our water. Not only that: to come in and buy up the land. Your da's farm would have gone, Patch. Slevin is in a powerful enough position to do it. They've already started to take over our town councils, preparing the ground.'

Tara came back into the room. 'And that's why we revived the Alphabet Network.'

Her father nodded. 'And it will always be there, in case we have to use it again. You see, Katie and Tom, you've saved Ireland. I needed this piece of evidence; our First Minister couldn't act on what I said about Slevin, because we had no proof. And it's just in time: the agreement between Slevin and that hoodlum is due to be signed tomorrow.'

Tara handed her father a piece of paper. 'An immediate response.'

```
My dear old friend,

The evidence I needed — and just in
time: my supporters have been wavering,
and that rogue Slevin has a strong
power-base. This will stop him once and
for all.

Your friend,

Brian
```

And Grandfather enfolded Katie and Tom in his arms in front of the fire.

'And now, let's sit down and eat!'

They all sat down at the long table — Grandfather and Tara; Katie, Tom and Patch; Willie, the boatman, and Mrs Kenny, who looked after Grandfather and Tara. Mrs Kenny had prepared all the food: cold chicken, ham, sausages, big bowls of potato salad, tarts, scones, chocolate, strawberry cake, pots of tea and jugs of hot chocolate.

'I won't be able to get on my horse in the morning,' laughed Patch. 'I'll be too heavy for the poor old thing. What a great tea!'

'There's a price,' said Tara.

'And what's that?' asked Patch.

'You're to do a party piece!'

So Patch took out his mouth-organ and played a few lively tunes, and then Grandfather and Tara sang a duet.

Katie looked embarrassed. 'I don't know anything.'

'I know!' shouted Tom. 'You can help me with my card tricks!' He dug a hand into his pocket, pulled out the cards and put them on the table.

Suddenly there was a high-pitched buzzing sound, and a thin red beam of light hit the pack. Tom and Katie screamed, and Patch leapt off his chair; but the others remained perfectly still, looking on as the pack of cards crumbled into a handful of dust.

Grandfather smiled at Tara. 'Well, I'm glad to see that our anti-bug device is working. Tom, where did you get those cards?' He reached out and gently took Tom's trembling hand in his.

'The — the ticket collector, at the beginning of our journey. He gave them to us. Ugh, I didn't like him one bit. I suppose I shouldn't have taken them, but I love cards, and —'

'It's all right, Tom, you weren't to know.' His grandfather sighed. 'Tartarus are very cunning. That's how they were able to track you all the way across Ireland: there was a tracking device in your card-pack.'

He looked over at Katie. 'Katie, dear, you're miles away. Don't worry: they can't do any more harm.'

Katie shook her head. 'I know, but talking about the ticket collector reminded me of Jane and Jack. Grandfather, do you think I could have a wish?'

Grandfather's green eyes twinkled. 'Anything you want. You deserve it.'

Katie looked at Tom. 'I — we — want Jack and Jane to come to Ireland, even if it's just for a holiday. I've got their address.'

Grandfather nodded. 'Of course. And now, I want to hear about all your adventures, right from the beginning.'

So they all settled down in front of the roaring fire, and Katie and Tom began their story.